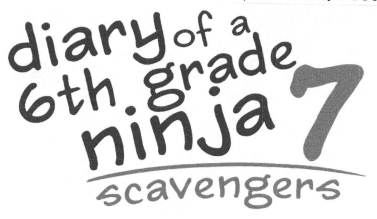

diary of a 6th grade ninja 7

scavengers

BY MARCUS EMERSON
AND NOAH CHILD

ILLUSTRATED BY DAVID LEE

EMERSON PUBLISHING HOUSE

So there I was falling into an ice volcano on Scrag Seven, one of Jupiter's undiscovered moons, with about a hundred ice-ninjas trailing behind me. I couldn't say I knew I'd be fine when I jumped into the volcano, but what I would say is this – I was glad that I changed into clean underwear that morning.

Oh, and don't for one second think I was in the middle of lunch, dreaming that insane scenario. *One time* that happened, and suddenly *I'm* the dude who falls asleep all the time? C'mon, people! Does that even *sound* like something I'd do?

…don't answer that.

No way was I asleep and dreaming. No way at all. Dreams aren't that cool!

My name is Chase Cooper, and I'm a sixth grade ninja… falling into an ice volcano on Scrag Seven.

The ice-ninjas had chased me across the frozen terrain of Scrag. They surprise attacked me when I was rescuing a girl they had imprisoned named Gwen. She was also a sixth grader. I don't know how she managed to get herself caught on one of Jupiter's moons, but she did. She was cute too, and totally had the hots for me because I'm a way cool ninja.

As Gwen and I fell deeper into the volcano, I spun around in the air. I wasn't sure exactly how many ice-ninjas were after us, but I knew we were stupidly outnumbered, and the floor of the volcano was coming up fast.

"Chase!" Gwen shouted. "The ground!"

I flipped over, grabbing Gwen's belt and pulling her closer.

1

"Hang on," I said.

With my right leg, I spun a roundhouse kick so lightning fast that our descent almost instantly stopped inches from the ground, allowing me to set my feet down as if I were simply stepping off a staircase. *Science!*

"Whoa," Gwen whispered, looking into my eyes. But her lovesick gaze quickly turned to fear as she looked above us. "*Look out!*"

From the reflection in her eyes, I could see a massive chunk of ice plummeting toward us. I dove into Gwen, pushing her out of harm's way, totally saving her life at the last second like it was a movie.

If it was just the chunk of ice, we would've been in the clear, but that would've been too easy. The ice-ninjas were about to drop around us at any moment.

I sighed, shaking my head. "Better stand back. It's about to get all kinds'a hot in here."

The thing about an army of ice-ninjas is that it doesn't take much to get rid of them. A simple flame would do, but being a fan of theatrics, I go with something a little… bigger.

Rounding my hands together like I was holding an invisible ball, I curled my body around. At that instant, a spark erupted at the center of my invisible ball. Continuing to move my hands rapidly, I contained the spark, pushing it around and around until it became a tiny flame. Then I blew into the center of the circle, right on the small ball of fire I had created.

The itty bitty ball of fire exploded before me, but luckily, my ninja master had taught me how to contain a blast like that. He also taught me how to *throw* a blast like that.

Shooting both of my hands above Gwen and me, the inferno surged from my fingertips.

The ice-ninjas tried to stop their descent, but it was too late. The ball of fire blew through them, instantly melting their frozen

3

bodies, sending them to their watery graves.

"How awful," Gwen said as small drops of water rained down upon us.

"They're not real," I said. "Just frozen water that the Scrag queen cast a spell on. They feel neither pain nor remorse."

"Still," Gwen said. "It's an awful fate."

"Better than rotting away in an ice-prison," I replied. Looking farther into the volcano's cavern, I said, "You've been here for awhile now. Any idea where the queen is?"

When I looked at Gwen's face, she was staring at me. Not angry. Just staring.

Her voice became a whisper. "Perhaps she's been with you the entire time…"

"What are you—" I started to say, but stopped when I turned around. The innocent little girl I had rescued was standing before me, her eyes glowing white as her hair flapped in the cold wind of the cavern. "Of course. My gut *told* me you couldn't be trusted."

"Then why did you?" the queen asked, her voice sounding like several voices speaking at once.

"Because," I said, shrugging a shoulder. "I just thought my gut was *hungry*."

The queen took a step closer to me. Her foot sizzled on the icy floor of the volcano as the cave started to rumble slightly. Specks of dust shook from the walls of the cavern, which meant the volcano was going to erupt… and it was going to erupt *soon*.

"I have to admit," the queen hissed, "you've made it *farther* than I ever expected. I figured by this time, I'd be sitting in front of my fireplace with buttered toast and a steaming cup of hot chocolate."

I thought the cave rumbled again, but it was just my stomach. Buttered toast and hot chocolate sounded *awesome*.

The queen continued. "*Join* me, Chase! *Join* me, and together we shall rule the human race!"

"Not a chance," I said. "I don't do well with public speaking, and if I ruled the human race, I'm sure I'd have to make, like, announcements and stuff."

The queen's eyes glowed brighter. "Then if you're not with me, you're against me!"

4

The light coming from the queen was so brilliant that I had to turn away. The temperature in the cavern dropped about a hundred degrees from cold to *way colder*. Any bit of moisture in my breath froze the instant it left my mouth, turning into microscopic specks of ice that fell to the floor. That could happen right? Yeah, that could *totally* happen.

The walls of the cavern shook again, this time more violently. Huge chunks of ice broke from above, smashing into the floor and shattering into millions of dangerously sharp pieces.

Trails of steam burst from cracks in the cavern, filling the cave with an icy fog. I started to wonder if I was going to make it out alive at all.

Forcing myself to look at the queen, I saw that she was powering up.

This was it. This was the queen's finishing move for the human race.

She'll create a blast powerful enough to cut across the solar system. All of humanity will become enslaved if I didn't do something to stop her.

"Knock it off!" I shouted, trying to step forward. It was difficult to move because the force of the queen's power was pushing against me.

"It's too late, Chase!" the queen shouted. "The storm is not coming! It is already here!"

I would've tried shooting another burst of fire, but the cavern was so cold that it was impossible to generate a spark fast enough. There was only one option left…

I'd have to tackle her.

But I knew the force of the queen's blast would eradicate *both* of us. What choice did I have? The only way to save Earth… was to *sacrifice* myself.

The queen arched her head back, focusing her power directly over her head.

Stumbling forward, I realized I wasn't being held back by her invisible energy anymore. With every ounce of strength I could muster, I sprinted at the queen through the violently shaking cavern.

"*What are you doing?*" the queen shouted.

More chunks of ice fell to the floor, exploding before me as I ran across the cavern, gunning for the evil queen of Scrag. "This one's for you, Earth!" I hollered.

As I jumped through the air, the ice volcano finally erupted. Huge pillars of ice broke through the floor of the cavern as the walls cracked apart.

My world turned to white as I made contact with the queen, smashing into her. A flash of intense pain flooded my body, but then it was gone…

Everything… was gone.

The human race was safe from enslavement by the queen of Scrag. I had done my duty as a ninja… as the defender of mankind, and the hero of—

"…cheeseburger." a girl's voice said.

I shook my head, embarrassed. The voice had come from my cousin, Zoe, who was seated on the bench next to me. The rest of my friends were hovering around the table, chuckling to themselves.

"What?" I asked, confused.

Zoe smirked with the side of her mouth. "I asked if you were feeling okay. You didn't even touch your cheeseburger."

"Yeah," I said, wiping my mouth, hoping there wasn't any drool. "I'm fine."

"It's just that I've been watching you for about five minutes," Zoe said. "And I don't think you've blinked once during

7

that time."

I scratched the back of my head. "Um, I was just thinking."

Told you I wasn't asleep and dreaming. I was just *daydreaming*.

"I didn't say anything, did I?" I asked.

"Nope," Gavin said. "But every couple seconds, your eyebrows twitched, like you were *gonna* say something angry, but never did."

"That happened *several* times," Faith laughed.

I exhaled deeply, sitting up straight. "What time is it? Is lunch over?"

"Yup," Zoe said. "The assembly's gonna start in a few. I wanted to come grab you before it did since we're not sitting with the rest of the other students."

"We're not?" I said, scooping my book bag off the floor. "Where are we sitting?"

"I'll be at the front of the gymnasium," Zoe explained. "You'll be nearby since you're my campaign manager."

"That's right," I said, shaking my head and returning to Earth.

Buchanan School was holding an emergency election to find a new president. The old president, Sebastian, was removed from office.

It's literally been three days since Sebastian was busted for trying to pull a fast one over the students and staff at Buchanan School. He lost his position as president, and Principal Davis felt like *that* was enough of a punishment so Sebastian was never suspended. He didn't even get detention!

All Sebastian had to do was issue an apology in the school's newspaper. That was it! I guess kids with power barely get a slap on the wrist when they get in trouble.

Earlier in the morning, Principal Davis announced an emergency election at the end of the week, hoping to keep morale up. But looking at the students around the cafeteria, it seemed like no one really cared that Buchanan didn't have a president at the moment.

It was Monday, and an assembly had been planned to take place after lunch that the entire sixth student body was attending. The candidates running for president were going to address the school. I wasn't sure who else was running yet, except for my cousin, who asked me to be her campaign manager.

Being the awesome relative I am, I said yes. Or maybe I said yes because I was only half listening to her when she asked. I had just found some emerald ore in a video game, and I *had* to mine it! Can you blame me? *Do you know how hard it is to find emerald ore?* It's like finding a *unicorn!*

Anyways, that's how I became Zoe's campaign manager. No bigs though, since I thought it'd be awesome if she became Buchanan School's president. She'd actually be the first *female* president the school has ever had. You'd think after a hundred years, Buchanan School would've seen at least *one* female president, but nope.

If you've kept up with my story, then you'll also remember the skeevy note I got from the Scavengers less than a week ago. All it said was that I had crossed a line and had awoken a sleeping giant. And then it said that the storm is not coming, but that it was already here, which was probably why the queen of Scrag screamed it at me.

I only learned about the existence of the Scavengers a week ago when Naomi told me about the rumor. Naomi was a valued member of my ninja clan, but she had also turned out to be a great friend. I'm not sure what I would do without her.

Nobody knows who the Scavengers are or even if they existed for sure. Supposedly they're some kind of secret organization within the school – so secret that people believe they're just a story to scare students.

I don't know though. I've been attending Buchanan for a few months now, and I've never seen any evidence of them. But that doesn't mean they *don't* exist. Ninety-nine percent of the kids at the school had no idea there were ninjas training in secret either.

I expected to hear from the Scavengers again over the weekend, but I didn't. I even thought maybe they'd mess with me earlier in the morning, but they also didn't do that.

I was beginning to think that maybe Wyatt had sent the note. It sounded like something he'd do to just to get into my head.

Wyatt, in case you didn't know, is the leader of the red ninja clan. He formed the new clan after his old clan kicked him out. The old clan appointed me as their new leader. Through some

9

shady actions, Wyatt had also become the vice president of Buchanan School. He even wore a sash with the words "VICE PRESIDENT" on it. Lame-o.

Thankfully, after Sebastian was booted from being president, Wyatt *wasn't* allowed to take his place. Principal Davis suspected some foul play, even though he couldn't completely prove anything.

So instead, the principal simply hit the "reset" button on the whole shabang.

Oh, and also as a side note, I still have no clue who the white ninja is. A few weeks ago, the white ninja saved me from getting served a bowl of drop-kick soup by a bunch of Wyatt's red ninjas. And then saved me *again* from them during the talent show. Both times, I never found out who it was, and I haven't seen him since. Part of my brain is starting to think that the ghost of James Buchanan sent an angel in the form of a ninja to rescue me. But maybe not though – that seemed a bit farfetched.

After pulling my book bag over my shoulders, I joined Zoe and my friends in the front lobby. Students were flowing through the halls, making their way to the gymnasium so they could find a seat for the assembly.

"Am I getting paid for this?" I asked Zoe.

"For being my manager?" Zoe said. "No. It's volunteer!"

"But is it a *paid* volunteer position?"

Zoe stopped in the hallway, folding her arms. "Volunteer means you don't get paid. Maybe you're the wrong guy for the job."

"No!" I laughed. "I'm kidding! I know what volunteer means! I was just messing with you!"

"Really?" Zoe asked. "Because this kind of sounds like something you'd actually be confused about."

"Really," I said. "And for the record, I'm happy to be part of this with you. You're gonna win this election so hard!"

"Right?" Faith said, clenching her fists in front of her. If her smile were a shining light, you'd be able to see it from space. "This is all so exciting! When you're president, I want you to relocate the vending machines that are in the lower levels of the school back into the cafeteria! I *hate* going into the dungeon to get a bag of spicy fries."

10

The dungeon was what students called the lower level of the school. I say "lower level" because it's not deep enough to be considered a basement. The whole level is probably about half a story underground, but it's still cold, dark, and wet, which was why it was called the dungeon. There *also* might be a dragon living down there. They say, late at night, you can hear the beast snoring, but I'm willing to bet it's just the heater kicking into gear.

"I'm not president yet," Zoe said to Faith. "But if I'm elected, I'll do my best about those machines."

"Whoa, whoa, whoa," Gavin, Zoe's boyfriend, said. "That's *after* you make sure they re-open the pool."

"What pool?" I asked. "We have a pool?"

"Yep," Gavin said. "Buchanan's got a bonafied Olympic sized swimming pool that's been shut down for years."

"*Weird*," I said. "It's probably a pretty dangerous place, right? And quiet too?"

My friends groaned when they realized what joke I was about to make.

"Dangerous and quiet… just like a ninja fart," I said. "Silent, but deadly."

"There it is," Zoe said, clapping her hands softly.

Everyone joined her golf-clap while staying stone-faced.

"It's funny!" I laughed.

"Keep telling yourself that," Faith said. "Maybe if you say it enough times, it'll *become* funny."

Zoe looked at Brayden, who was walking at the end of our line. "And what about you? Any special requests from you?"

"Not exactly," Brayden smiled. "I was going to keep this from you guys, but I've decided to run too."

"Are you serious?" Faith asked.

I thought Zoe was going to get upset with Brayden, but she surprised me.

My cousin's eyes lit up. "That's cool! Are you going to introduce any monster-hunting classes if you get elected?"

Brayden was a self-proclaimed monster hunter. He swore there were werewolves running around the hills of northern Wisconsin, and has devoted his life to finding one. He was even the founder of a popular website where people could post their crazy monster theories to message boards. So far, there were only

11

three members – Brayden, his mom, and me. Yeah, it's pretty sad.

"Actually," Brayden said. "I think I'm gonna go easy on the 'monster-hunter' thing during my run. A lot of kids are afraid of what they don't know, and I'm pretty sure they don't know anything about monster hunting. If that little bit about me came out, then I'd lose the election for sure."

Faith chuckled. "You hear that, Zoe? You can run a smear campaign against Brayden. That would just make one less candidate for you to worry about."

"I'm *not* running a smear campaign," Zoe said. "That's not the way I'd want to win. Besides, Brayden and I are friends. He wouldn't do that to me either." Zoe paused. "Would you?"

"Never!" Brayden said. He stepped up to the gymnasium doors. "See you guys on the flipside."

After Brayden disappeared behind the gym doors, Gavin spoke. "See you on the flipside? Did we time travel back to the 80's?"

We all laughed.

Faith and Gavin said goodbye, and headed down the hallway, to where the other students were entering the gym. Brayden had used the door that only the students running for office were allowed to use. And their campaign managers.

I held the door open for my cousin. "Age before beauty."

"I'm, like, a month older than you," Zoe said. "And are you calling yourself beautiful?"

"No," I said, tripping over my words. "I just… I mean… um…"

"Relax," Zoe sighed. "Don't hurt your brain too much. I'll need it in one piece since you're managing my campaign."

Following my cousin through the door, we both entered the gymnasium.

Monday. 12:25 PM. The gymnasium.

Most of the students from Buchanan were already there, sitting in the bleachers along both ends of the room. I'm not sure why, but the sound of hundreds of kids talking to each other felt calming.

Zoe took the lead, walking down one end of the bleachers. "As my campaign manager, do you know what your responsibilities are?"

"Yes," I said with full confidence. "But just in case, you should tell me anyways."

Zoe grunted, frustrated. "You're in charge of everything that's related to my campaign. Scheduling speeches, autograph signings, baby kissings, and so on."

"You want me to set up a baby kissin' booth?" I joked.

"Creepy much?" Zoe replied. "You need to be the one who makes the posters and puts them up all over the school. You'll also be in charge of trying to encourage kids to vote for me."

"Isn't getting votes *your* job?"

"Yes, but you'll help too. You can hand out buttons between classes that say 'Vote for Zoe' or something catchier than that." Zoe glanced at me over her shoulder. "You'll also figure out how various groups of students feel about me."

"What do you mean?"

"Like, do the hipsters agree with my school views? Are the jocks leaning for or against me? Am I doing well with the orchestra students? If not, how can I win their votes? Those sorts of things."

"Gotcha," I said.

"Kay," Zoe said. "I'll need you to start thinking of some great quotes for my acceptance speech, y'know, if I *do* win on Friday."

"Quotes?" I asked. "How about something like 'Dance like no one's watching?'"

My cousin's face scrunched up. "Sick, dude. These aren't a bunch of fairytale cartoon princesses I'm speaking to. These are *real* kids who have heard that same quote a billion different ways. Gimme something better!"

I chewed my lip for a moment. "How about, 'Dance like *everyone's* watching?'"

Zoe slugged my shoulder, the same doggone spot she did every time! I bet my bone structure was starting to take a different shape from getting punched in the same place for so long.

"Make it something about leadership," Zoe snipped.

"Fine," I said, rubbing my arm. "I guess if I looked at myself, I'd like to think I was a good leader because I never cared about being better than the other guy. It's about always trying to be better than *yourself*."

Zoe gave me puppy dog eyes. She whistled as she started scribbling in a notebook. "That's a good one," she said. "I'm *so* using that if I win."

"Sure," I said. "It's not like I'll be using it."

"And don't forget about tomorrow!" Zoe said.

I hesitated. "What's tomorrow?"

Zoe's shoulder slumped as a worried look filled her eyes. "Please tell me you're joking again."

I tried to put up a poker face, but couldn't. "You know I am, boss! Tomorrow's pizza party is all set. I've got fifty pizzas on deck for delivery during lunch tomorrow."

Zoe's nose wrinkled as she smiled. "Good."

Want to know how awesome my cousin is? She's putting on a pizza party *buffet* for the entire sixth grade student body at Buchanan during lunch. And the best part? It's *totally* free for kids. All you have to do is show up, grab a plate, and grab some 'za, which is what my dad calls pizza. She's calling it a "free-za party." Pronounce free-za the way you would pizza. That's how you say it.

It's going to cost a lot of money, but Zoe is paying for the whole thing. Unlike me, she's been saving every penny of her allowance since she was five, waiting for the perfect thing to spend it on. I don't think she had to think twice about spending it on her campaign. And kids are going to go *nuts* about it too. This "random act of awesome" might be all she needed to win the election.

From the corner of my eye, I saw a flash of light, and then heard a "*poomph*" sound.

"Perfect!" said a boy's voice.

Zoe and I stopped to see who was talking to us. Briskly walking in our direction was a shorter kid, holding a giant camera that looked like it was from the 1930's – the kind with the big metal bowl on top that held the flashbulb.

He was wearing dark brown khaki pants and a brown suit coat complete with a brown tie. On top of his head was a fedora with a slip of paper tucked into the strap that had the word

15

"PRESS" on it. He frowned, as he approached.

"Thank ya, kindly!" the boy said. "Now can I get one of the two of you together?"

"Who're you?" I asked, stepping in front of my cousin so the kid couldn't take another photograph of her.

"Calm yourself, lad," the boy said. "I'm just a reporter. I'm documenting the election for the school paper. The name's Melvin."

MELVIN

"It's alright, Chase," Zoe said, gently pushing me aside. "Melvin's just doing his job."

Melvin sighed. "Trust me, I *wish* I were reporting a story that was more exciting, but my editor said I had to be here, so I am."

"What's more exciting than an election?" Zoe asked, smiling like a movie star.

The reporter didn't hesitate. "*Ninjas*," he replied, zeroing

16

his eyes in on me.

"No such thing," Zoe said immediately, sounding slightly nervous. "At least at Buchanan. I mean, ninjas existed centuries ago in feudal Japan, but that's about it."

I wasn't sure if Melvin looked at me because he knew I was a ninja or if his stare was just a coincidence. Either way, it had me kinda freaked. "Ninjas? What're you talking about?" I asked, hoping I sounded genuine.

Melvin smacked his lips together. "Lotta nasty rumors about a ninja runnin' around here. Plus there was that picture in the paper a couple months ago. Hall monitors ain't found the kid yet."

Melvin was referring to an article in the school paper from awhile back. There was a picture on the front page of a ninja stealing someone's stuff. The ninja was wearing black robes, which also happened to be *my* robes.

Let me explain – a couple months ago, Wyatt stole my book bag. It was before I wore my ninja outfit under my street clothes, so my outfit was *inside* the bag. In an effort to ruin my week, Wyatt ran around Buchanan wearing *my* ninja uniform, wreaking havoc on anyone within a five-foot radius of him. The school paper caught wind of this, snapped that photo, and claimed there was a ninja among us.

Most of the students have moved on from that rumor, but apparently *Melvin* had not.

"That photo was a fake, y'know," I said. "There aren't any ninjas in the school."

Melvin's brow tightened. "*I* took that photo," he said coldly. "I was *there*, man. I *saw* that ninja with my own two eyes."

Zoe came to my rescue, changing the subject. She put her arm over my shoulder. "Didn't you want a pic?"

Melvin lifted his humongous camera. "Smile!"

Zoe smiled like a champ. I did my best to fake one. The bulb above Melvin's camera went off, making the "*poomph*" sound again as a ball of smoke appeared above it.

I rubbed my eyes. It was the brightest flash I'd ever seen in my life. I wouldn't be surprised if the front part of my brain got singed from it.

"Good luck with the election," Melvin said as he walked past us.

17

"Weird, kid," I said.

"I know weirder," Zoe smirked. "You worried about the ninja thing?"

"Nah," I said. "We've gone this long without being discovered. We'll be fine."

Monday. 12:35 PM. The gymnasium.

Zoe was at the front of the gym, sitting next to Brayden in metal foldout chairs. They were the first two candidates to take their spot on the basketball court. The other two candidates weren't with them yet.

Principal Davis stood in front of a podium, constantly checking his watch and tapping his foot. Every couple seconds, he would look up from his wrist and shake his head.

I was standing off to the side of the gym next to a set of bleachers. Naomi had found me and decided to stand by my side instead of sitting with the other students.

"Excuse me!" came a small voice from behind us. "I'm running late!"

I was surprised to see a petite girl with blonde hair jet past me. She was about half a foot shorter than me, with very pale skin, but not gross pale – more like porcelain doll pale. Cute too.

Naomi nudged my side with her elbow. "Keep your eyes to yourself, tiger."

I let out a laugh through my nose. "What're you talking about?" I joked, acting like I had no idea what Naomi was talking about.

After the girl ran past us, she made her way to the area where the candidates were seated. She took the spot on the other side of Zoe, smiling and catching her breath.

Principal Davis nodded as he said something to her. She laughed and gave him a thumbs-up.

Someone else spoke behind Naomi and me again, but this time it was a gruff voice. "Step aside, children."

I turned around, not surprised to see Jake and his wolf pack.

Let me tell you a little bit about Jake. He's the cool kid in school, I'm sure there's someone at *your* school that's the same as him, but just a different model number. Star quarterback, cheerleader girlfriend, and friends with a bunch of kids who are either good looking or super beefy jocks.

The kids who always tagged along with Jake were known as his wolf pack, because wolves that travel together are referred to as just that – a wolf pack. Plus they got their name before the school changed mascots from the Wildcats to the Moose.

Jake has also had his sights set on me for awhile, especially now though because of what happened a week earlier at the career fair. Long story short – he chased me down, but with some help from some good friends, I got away... but not before Jake got painted up as a circus clown for the whole school to scoff at.

I took a couple steps back so Jake and his thugs could get through.

Jake glared at me as he passed, but I knew he wasn't going to try anything – not in the gymnasium filled with students and teachers. That didn't stop him from shoulder checking me against the wall though. And in the same spot that Zoe had slugged me.

Thankfully that was it. Jake and his wolf pack climbed the bleachers until they were on the very top row, so they could heckle the students under them.

I looked back at the kids running for president. There was only one more empty seat at the front of the gym, which meant there was still one candidate everyone was waiting for.

All of a sudden, the gym lights flickered off. Everyone in the room gasped at the same time, but their moment of surprise turned into a mob of shouts and cheers. It was a pretty typical reaction from a bunch of sixth graders going wild when the power goes out.

Their shouts stopped when a crack of thunder shock-waved through the room. The sound had come from the speaker system, which meant Buchanan still had power and that the lights had purposefully been switched off.

A voice spoke through the speakers. "Ladies and gentlemen,

prepare yourselves for greatness! Your eyes will tear up at the sight of him! Your ears will pop at the wisdom that drips from his lips! Your hearts will melt at his dapper demeanor. Your brains will be blown from his philosophical school views. Guys and gals, please welcome, the *next* president of Buchanan School! *Wyaaaaaaaaatt!*"

A spotlight switched on, pointing at the center of the basketball court, where Wyatt was standing with his arms in the air waving to the students in the bleachers. He was sporting a smug grin, which just made the whole charade feel weird and creepy.

Then Wyatt stomped his foot on the floor, which was the signal for the DJ to start playing techno music. As electronic music poured through the speakers, Wyatt spun in a circle and started *moonwalking* toward the podium.

None of the sixth graders applauded for him, but I don't think it was because they didn't like him. I think it was more because we were all shocked and confused at what was happening.

Wait, I take that back – *one* student was standing at attention, clapping like a maniac the way a baby does when they first learn how to slap their hands together. It was Olivia Jones, Wyatt's girlfriend.

Wyatt continued his moonwalk across the gym, but it was obvious that he was getting tired. His smooth motions became jagged and robotic. I guess he shouldn't have started so far from the podium. Watching him was the most painful thirty seconds of my life. I kinda felt sorry for the kid.

At long last, he made it to the podium. The lights in the gym flickered back to life as he took a seat on the other side of the petite blonde girl. His chest was heaving up and down from heavy breathing.

Principal Davis tapped on the mic. "I'd like to thank everyone for skipping their classes for the last half of the day."

The gymnasium full of sixth graders chuckled quietly at his joke.

"But seriously," the principal continued. "We're here today to meet the four students who are running for class president. There's a camera in the back recording the assembly so the homeschooled kids in our district will be able to watch the speeches from their houses. Don't forget that they're invited to cast their vote as well. After my short introduction, each of the candidates will make their speech. After that, the rest of the assembly is set aside for a question and answer session. Don't hesitate to ask the tough questions here. They're expecting that. So please, if you will, give our candidates a round of applause!"

I whistled through my fingers as everyone clapped their hands and cheered.

Principal Davis turned halfway around and held his open hand out to each candidate as he introduced them. "Give a hand to Wyatt, Daisy, Zoe, and Brayden!"

Daisy was the petite girl's name, huh? I don't know why, but it seemed fitting for her.

The principal stepped away from the podium as he gestured to the four students running for president. I saw him mouth the words, "The floor is yours."

DAISY

Wyatt was the first to step up to the podium. He flipped through a few index cards, squinting his eyes like he was having a tough time reading his own handwriting. Finally, he tossed the cards over his head.

With both hands, he gripped the sides of the podium and leaned into the microphones. He paused for dramatic effect. "I know I haven't been the greatest kid in the world," he started.

Olivia shouted from the bleachers. "It's alright, babe! We all deserve second chances!"

Wyatt smirked, pointing his finger at his girlfriend. "Not all of us, sweetie. I know for a fact that a lot of students don't like me, and I don't blame them."

Then Olive stood, pumping her fist in the air, trying to start a chant. "*Wy-att, Wy-att, Wy-att!*"

Nobody joined her. Around the tenth time saying "Wy-att," she finally fizzled out and returned to her seat.

Wyatt cleared his throat. "I don't blame anyone if they feel anger towards me."

I folded my arms. What was he trying to say?

"At the beginning of the year," Wyatt went on, "I tried

framing another student for stealing money from the food drive, and I've realized recently, that I've never apologized." Wyatt turned around with puppy dog eyes and looked at Zoe. "So I'd like to start my speech… by saying I'm sorry. Truly I am."

The crowd fell silent as they watched Zoe, waiting for her reaction.

Zoe returned with a genuine smile. "I appreciate that, Wyatt. I accept your apology."

I knew my cousin would – she doesn't have a vengeful bone in her body, unless there's some kind of mysterious bone actually called "vengeful." I don't think there is, but don't take my word for it. I ain't a doctor.

Wyatt turned back to the microphone. After another dramatic pause, he spoke. "There's a good number of kids who see me as the bad guy, with good reason too. But I'm here to say that nobody ever sees *themselves* as the bad guy. Let me explain – do you think I walk the halls of our beautiful school with the intent of being evil? Do you think I wake up in the morning and wonder what kind of terror I could muster up for the day?"

"Yes," I muttered quietly.

Naomi slowly exhaled, her eyes focused on the leader of the red ninja clan.

"The point is that I'm *not* a bad guy," Wyatt said. "I'm more like the *misunderstood* guy. Isn't everyone though? I'm a *victim* of labeling, and I'm here to tell you that labeling someone is just as bad as bullying someone. After enough time, the guy who's labeled will start *acting* like his label. Students, I'm here, standing before you in our beautiful school, to admit that I've messed up in the past. I know I don't deserve a second chance, but I'm *asking* if you'd give me one. I'm proof that kids can change, and a vote for me shows that we're *all* capable of change."

I couldn't help but chuckle. Who did this kid think he was? What has he *changed* since the beginning of the year? It was the most ridiculous speech I'd ever heard, and I knew that the rest of the school wasn't going to fall for *any* of it!

As if the universe wanted to prove me wrong, the crowd of students cheered for Wyatt.

"Wow, seriously?" I said aloud.

But Wyatt wasn't finished. He pounded his fist on the

podium and spoke loudly. "And my first act, if elected to president, will be to change our absurd mascot to something way cooler than a dopey moose! We deserve better than that, and I'm going to make sure we get it!"

At that statement, everyone hollered again.

Buchanan's old mascot was a wildcat up until I changed it to a moose. Yes, it was my idea. No, I wasn't proud of it. If I could take it back, I totally would, but the ball was already rolling when I realized everyone hated it, like, *passionately* hated it.

Wyatt raised both hands in the air, holding out the first two fingers on each one, the universal signal for "victory." He moonwalked back to his metal chair with his arms up the whole time.

Next, Daisy took the stage. She cleared her throat, but before I could hear any of her speech, someone tapped on my shoulder.

Mrs. Robinson, my homeroom teacher, was standing behind me with her hand keeping the door to the gym open. "I'm sorry to bother you," she said, "but you're needed in the front office."

"Is something wrong?" I asked nervously.

"No, nothing like that," Mrs. Robinson said. "There's just a package waiting for you there."

"A package?" Naomi repeated. "Who gets a *package* at school?"

"It's not uncommon," the teacher said. "Sometimes parents drop things off for their kids during the day."

"Is it from my parents?" I asked.

Mrs. Robinson rolled her eyes, clearly annoyed at all our questions. "I have no idea. All it says is your name on it."

"How big is it?" I asked, hoping that maybe my parents had dropped off a next-gen console for me to unwrap. Hey, I can *hope*, can't I?

"*For the love of—*" my homeroom teacher grumbled. "Just get to the front office and pick it up, wouldya?"

Mrs. Robinson pushed open the door, and disappeared.

Naomi pointed to the candidates on the floor. "What about Zoe? Don't you need to be here for her? You're her campaign manager."

I glanced at my cousin, who was sitting in her chair,

listening to Daisy's speech. Even though Naomi was right, what kid *couldn't* resist getting a package at school? I walked to the door and pushed the metal handlebar down. "It won't take long. Zoe doesn't need me during her speech. I'll be back before the question and answer session."

"Oh no you don't," Naomi said. "You mean '*we'll*' be back, don't you?"

"Yes," I said with a smile. "That's exactly what I meant.

Monday. 12:50 PM. The front offices.

A few minutes later, Naomi and I were standing at the counter of the front office. Most of the staff was in the gym listening to speeches of the four candidates, but the nurse was still in the room.

"Can I help you?" Nurse Duvall asked.

"Mrs. Robinson said there was a package for me?" I stated. "The name's Cooper. *Chase* Cooper."

"Been watching spy movies lately?" Naomi whispered, leaning back on the counter like she didn't care.

"*Maybe*," I answered.

Nurse Duvall fumbled with something behind the counter. Then she set a small cardboard box in front of me. "Here it is," she said.

I studied the box for a moment. It was about the size of a thick textbook, which meant my parents did *not* drop off a next-gen console, even *after* all the hints I'd been dropping.

"Thanks," I said to the nurse as I lifted it off the counter.

Mrs. Duvall nodded, and waved me out the door.

Out in the lobby, I held the box close to my ear and shook it.

"Is it heavy?" Naomi asked.

"Nope," I said. "I hear something in there, don't you?"

Naomi rolled her eyes. "Pretty sure you wouldn't get any *empty* package delivered to you."

27

"What if it's a trap?" I asked.

"It's *not* a trap," Naomi said.

"But what if it is?" I asked again.

"It's *not*," Naomi repeated. "You think you're going to open that and a net's gonna fly out?"

I paused. "What if it's an *ear?*"

"An *ear*? A *human* ear? What's the *matter* with you?"

"You're right. It's probably not an ear," I said. "But maybe... *just* maybe... it *is*."

"Just open it already!" Naomi sighed.

Keeping the box in front of me, I took a seat on one of the benches in the lobby. Naomi sat next to me. I scraped my finger along the side of the small cardboard box, lifting the tape off the corner.

"Wait," Naomi said. "Now I'm worried this *is* a trap."

"Too late!" I laughed, pulling the cover of the cardboard apart.

There was a moment where I felt the same thrill that I do on Christmas morning, but that thrill disappeared when I saw what was inside. The only item the box contained was a vulture mask that looked more cartoony than scary. After I touched the mask, I noticed there were actually *two* masks in the box.

Naomi paused, studying the masks. "Soooooo... that's not somethin' you see everyday."

Removing the masks from the box, I checked to see if there was anything else inside. There wasn't.

"*Huh*," I grunted.

"Wait," Naomi said, touching her finger to the bottom of the two masks in my hands. She lifted them slightly. "There's something taped to the inside."

When I flipped them over, I saw a fancy cream-colored envelope. It was the same type of envelope my parents got when a wedding invitation came in the mail. The front of the casing even had the words "YOU'RE INVITED," written in cursive.

The top of the invitation wasn't sealed, so I flipped it open and took out the thick cardstock. The paper was smooth like velvet.

Naomi twitched when she saw it. I hadn't even read the invitation yet, but I already knew who it was from.

28

INVITATION

THE HONOR OF YOUR PRESENCE IS REQUESTED AT THE CELEBRATION OF OUR NEWEST MEMBER, CHASE COOPER.

MONDAY, ONE-O-CLOCK IN THE AFTERNOON. ROOM 001, IN THE DUNGEON. COOKIES AND DANCING TO FOLLOW.

THIS INVITATION IS FOR YOU PLUS ONE GUEST. ATTENDANCE IS COMPULSORY.

WE LOOK FORWARD TO SEEING YOU THERE. THE SCAVENGERS

CREEPY VULTURE MASK

*The honor of your presence is requested
at the celebration of our newest member, Chase Cooper.*

*Monday, one-o-clock in the afternoon.
Room 001, in the dungeon.
Cupcakes and dancing to follow.*

*This invitation is for you plus one guest.
Attendance is compulsory.*

*We look forward to seeing you there.
The Scavengers*

Naomi frowned, whispering, "*The Scavengers...*"
I tried to lighten the mood. "Seeing as how this is the *least* intimidating note I've ever received, I'm not too worried about it. I

mean, *look* at the paper quality! It's even got a shimmer to it! I'm willing to bet this is 110 lb. pearl white with 14 point thickness."

"Wow," Naomi said, raising her eyebrows. "I have *no idea* what any of that means."

"It means the Scavengers have spent some money to make this invitation," I said. "I don't think a secret club would invest in something like this if they meant any harm."

"Or, or, or," Naomi said quickly and sarcastically. "It means this secret club is that *delusional, psychotic,* and *dangerous* that they would declare war on someone in such a fashionable way!"

I set the masks back in the box, and then pulled my pants up as if I were getting ready for some grueling outdoor work. "Well, then," I said, doing my best 1800's farmer impression. "We best not lolly-gag and see what all the fuss is about, bein' as how we were on the recievin' end of such a fanciful summons."

"I'm not sure exactly what you just said, but it sounds like you're actually going into the dungeon to meet with these nut jobs."

"The invite says I can bring a guest," I said. "Wanna be my plus one?"

"No," Naomi replied. "But since you're probably not going to do the smart thing by staying away from there, I guess I'll *have* to accompany you."

"Atta girl," I joked.

At that, Naomi slugged my shoulder. She's been working hard to perfect her one-inch-punch, and she was getting darn good at it.

"Ow!" I said. "*Why* does everyone keep hitting that same spot? It's like you guys all studied a chart with my body on it and agreed to keep jabbing at the same spot over and over again until it falls off! That's something crazy monkeys would do! Is that why you're doing it? Did the crazy monkeys put you up to this?"

Naomi answered very seriously, as if it should've been obvious. "Yes."

Biting my lip, I acted like it didn't hurt. Then we started making our way to the lower level of Buchanan, also known as the dungeon.

This wasn't the smartest idea in the world, but deep down, I was excited at the thrill of experiencing something new.

Monday. 12:59 PM. Outside Room 001 in the dungeon.

Since most of the students and staff were still in the gymnasium listening to the speeches of the presidential candidates, Naomi and I had no trouble walking down to the lower level. It didn't take us more than a minute to get to the dungeon.

We stood outside room 001 and stared at the humongous wooden door. Hanging over the front of the door was a set of fake vines with leaves that were gently rustling. A broken water fountain directly behind us was pumping water out of its spigot.

"Do we knock?" Naomi asked.

"I guess," I said, unsure. "I hope there's not a secret phrase I need to know."

"Judging by the fact that you received an invite," Naomi said, "I'd bet they're expecting you."

I held the vulture masks in front of me. "Should we wear these, or our ninja masks?"

Naomi stared at the masks for a moment. "The Scavengers are expecting *you*, not a ninja. If we went there in our ninja outfits, I think the cat would get let out of the bag."

I shook my head. "Who's putting cats in bags anyways? Seems like a mean thing to do."

Naomi smiled.

I took a deep breath. "Worst case scenario? We go in and they say a bunch of mean things to us, right?"

"Negative," Naomi said. "The worst case scenario is that you die."

"Just me?" I asked. "Not you too?"

"No way," Naomi replied. "Because your death is going to be the distraction I'll use to escape. I'll be halfway to Tahiti before your funeral."

I knocked three times on the wooden door. From behind the entrance, I heard several quick whispers and some shuffling of feet. And then the door cracked open an inch, revealing a boy's eye. The eye darted back and forth between Naomi and me.

"Yes?" the boy asked through the slit.

I leaned closer, trying to get a better look at the kid behind the door, but the room was too dark. I held out my invitation so he could see it clearly. "I got this just a few minutes ago. It said I was invited to something in this room."

The door clunked shut.

"Welp, that's that!" Naomi said. "Can't say we didn't try! Let's get back to the gym. I bet Zoe's giving her speech by now."

Another clunking noise came from the door. After that, it slowly slid open, but not more than a few inches. The kids on the other side weren't going to pull the door open for us. They expected us to enter at our own risk.

"Don't," Naomi said. "Seriously, this is messed up. Let's just leave now."

I ignored Naomi's plea, pushing against the heavy door. It opened steadily. I tried to see what was inside, but the lights were out. It was dark, scary, and dangerous – three good reasons I should've walked away, but you know how curious I can be.

The fake leaves spread apart as I stepped through, making a "shhhhhhh" sound. It was like walking into a secret area of a video game.

Naomi grunted as she followed me into the mysterious room. "If we die, I'm gonna kill you."

As soon as we were a few feet inside the dark room, the door slammed shut behind us. I spun around, but couldn't see a thing. Because the room was in the lower level of Buchanan, there weren't any windows to let any sunlight in.

"Remember your training," I said to Naomi.

"I could be wrong, but I don't remember any training that involved stepping into a trap," Naomi said.

From the far side of the room, a voice spoke softly. "Welcome, Chase. We've been *expecting* you."

The long fluorescent bulbs flickered awake overhead, revealing a room full of kids wearing the same vulture masks that were inside the package I received. I almost felt scared until I saw one of the kids standing next to the light switch by the front door. I don't know why, but when I imagined him flipping the lights on, I felt less afraid. I think it's like a magic act – when you understand the truth about what you were seeing, all the *magic* disappears.

I was simply standing in a room full of kids wearing the same dumb vulture masks.

The room looked completely ordinary. There wasn't a strange thing about it except for the weirdoes staring at us through their Halloween costumes. Desks were lined in rows just like all the other classrooms in the buildings. Up front, the dry erase board had some notes scribbled on it, which meant the room was still used for class, just not at the moment.

"S'up," I said confidently. Holding up my invitation, I said, "So yeah, I got this in the front office. Is someone getting married down here?"

Naomi stood behind me. She straightened her posture when she realized I wasn't scared. She was brave when she saw my example. At that moment, I felt like a strong leader.

One of the taller students stepped closer, but not too close. "We've been watching you since the first week of school. You've been a strong blip on our radar that won't go away."

"I *do* go to school here, y'know," I said sarcastically. "Where am I gonna go?"

The boy ignored my remark. "You've shown amazing growth as the days have passed, which is why you've received our invitation."

I tossed the fancy cardstock onto one of the desks nearby. "What's this about?"

"Isn't it obvi?" the boy asked, shortening the word

34

"obvious" and using animated gestures as he spoke. It was almost like our conversation was music that he was dancing to. "This is because of your interference with Sebastian last week."

"Sebastian?" Naomi said. "What's he got to do with this? He's a Scavenger, isn't he?"

"*Was*," the masked boy said. "Sadly, he's no longer with us."

I gasped. "He's... *dead?*"

"*No, dude*," the boy said, annoyed. "I mean he's not a *Scavenger* anymore!"

"To be fair, *you* said that '*he wasn't with us anymore*' in a such a creepster way," I said. "Just sounded like he was dead."

"But that is why you're here with us," the boy said.

Everyone in the room stood silently, like mannequins in a store.

"Because I've awoken a sleeping giant," I said, repeating the words of the original note I received only a few days before. "The storm is already here, right?"

"You misunderstand," the boy said. "The simple fact that we've revealed ourselves to you shows that we should *not* be enemies. Rather, we should be working *together*. Never in the history of Buchanan has a Scavenger been taken down the way Sebastian was. You've shown true talent, and *that* is why you are with us today. You're the newest Scavenger. Congratulations."

I looked at Naomi. She shook her head at me.

"May we offer you an orange soda?" the Scavenger asked. "We know it's your favorite."

"Um," I said, a little confused. "No thanks."

The Scavenger pointed two fingers at Naomi. "How about you? You're Naomi, right? That means you like Tea. Earl Grey. Hot."

Naomi chewed her lip. "Yeah, that's my favorite drink, but... I think I'll pass."

"Your loss," the Scavenger sighed.

Across the room, another Scavenger holding our already prepared drinks sunk his shoulders like he was bummed that we didn't want them.

Naomi stepped forward. "What the heck are you guys? You've been nothing more than a rumor to the rest of the school, and now that I see you, I still don't understand the reason you guys even exist!"

Another one of the Scavengers stepped forward. She was shorter than the first, and had a very soft and feminine voice. "We are the Scavengers, and we know *everything* about *everyone*. There are no secrets the Scavengers don't know. We are everywhere and nowhere."

A voice started speaking across the room. One of the other kid's wearing a vulture mask took his turn talking. "Every conversation you've ever had has been listened to. Every note you've ever tossed in the garbage has been collected and documented. Every student in Buchanan has a file with the Scavengers. Every. Single. Student."

The girl in front spoke again. "Your ninja clan might be a secret to the school, but not to *us*."

I felt the air escape from my lungs. "I guess the cat was never *in* the bag," I wheezed to Naomi.

"We know *everything* about you, Chase," the girl said, and then started listing off intimate details of my life. "Your feud with Wyatt and his red ninja clan, your beef with Jake, the fact that Naomi and Brayden are members of your clan, your silly crush on Faith, your allergies to bees, your mild intolerance to lactose... we even know that your jaw sometimes clicks when you eat."

I stared at the girl in the vulture mask, shocked. "How is that possible?"

The Scavenger that first spoke when we entered the room crossed his arms. "We told you. We know *everything* about *everyone*."

"Oh yeah?" I asked, wanting to test them. "If you know everything about everyone, tell me who the white ninja is."

The boy in the mask paused. "Of course we know who it is, but that information is just for *Scavengers*."

"But why?" Naomi asked. "Why bother with so much useless information?"

"*We* are the ones in control of the school," the boy said. "*We* are the ones making the decisions around here. We've got the goods on everyone – the students, the staff, even many of the parents – and we know how to use that information to get what we want."

"You guys can't know *everything*," Naomi hissed. "It's not even possible to—"

The girl Scavenger spoke immediately, cutting Naomi off. "You've been a member of Chase's ninja clan since the beginning, before it was even *his*. Wyatt recruited you because you bullied a student simply because he was in '*your*' seat during lunch. You embarrassed him so bad that he still avoids eye contact with you."

"Naomi," I whispered. "Is this true?"

Naomi stared at the floor. "It's not something I'm proud of. It happened *before* you showed us what being a true ninja meant." Naomi's eyes returned to the Scavenger. "But that's information anyone would know – it happened in *front* of everyone. In front of—"

The girl spoke, interrupting my friend again. "You're jealous that Faith has caught Chase's eye because *you've* got a huge crush on him. For several weeks, you've been wondering if you should say something... but, how did you say it in your note to Zoe? You just 'can't find the courage to tell him.' Is that right? Zoe tossed the note into the garbage can in the girl's locker room. We simply... *collected* it."

Naomi fell silent. Her face was expressionless as she stared at the floor.

I was speechless, not just at the fact that Naomi had a thing for me, but because the Scavengers really *did* know everything.

The leader of the Scavengers stepped forward, speaking with animated gestures again. "No worries," he said. "Your secrets are safe with us, especially now that you're a member."

"But I'm *not* a—" I started say.

"We're excited to have you," he continued. "This might be a little quick, but there's no time to waste. Now that you're one of us, you'll have to *quit* your ninja clan. You can appoint a new leader if you want, but you can't say anything about your reason for quitting."

I tried to speak again, but the boy was talking too quickly.

"After that, you'll take the presidency since *you* were the one who removed Sebastian from office. You'll run, along with the other candidates, but you *will* win because *we'll* make sure of it."

"But my cousin is running," I said.

The boy paused, staring at me through the eyeholes in his

mask. "So?"

"So no!" I said angrily. "I'm not running against my cousin! I'm not quitting my ninja clan! And I'm sure as spew not joining your creepy little gang of garbage pickers!"

The boy adjusted his vulture mask. "I'm afraid the choice is *not* yours to make."

Naomi still stared at the ground. I felt awful for how embarrassed she must've felt.

"I make my own choices," I said. "And right now, I'm choosing to walk away from you. C'mon, Naomi."

I turned around and started for the door. I heard Naomi shuffle her feet behind me.

"We won't stop you from leaving," the Scavenger said loudly. "Because you can never get away from us. If you reject our offer, then be prepared for the whirlwind of disaster that's coming your way. And don't even *think* about telling anyone about us, or it'll mean your *complete* and *utter* destruction."

I glanced over my shoulder before stepping through the door. All I saw were a bunch of kids wearing goofy bird masks. What kind of harm were they actually capable of?

Without saying another word, I left the room. The door shut as Naomi dragged her feet out behind me.

"Sooooo," I said, again trying to lighten the mood. "Don't worry about all that in there, okay? I won't tell anyone that you've got a mega crush on the leader of your ninja clan."

I expected Naomi to laugh at my joke, but she didn't. Instead, she jogged down the hall, away from me. She didn't even respond to my comment.

"I shouldn't have said that," I whispered aloud. "Slick, Chase. Real slick."

Monday. 2:00 PM. The gymnasium.

After my meeting with the Scavengers, I went back to the gym to watch the rest of the speeches. Just outside the gym doors, I snapped the two vultures masks in half and chucked them into a garbage bin – no need to carry those ugly things around since I wasn't going to play their game.

I caught the tail end of Brayden's speech, which meant I completely missed Daisy and Zoe's speeches.

Brayden was more confident than I expected him to be, which was awesome. He promised an increase of art and music classes, along with funding for more school-trips throughout the year. The students responded pretty well to what he said. And not one time did he mention werewolves, vampires, or big foots.

The question and answer session was supposed to take place after the speeches, but didn't happen. The candidates waited for someone, *anyone*, to ask a question, but nobody did.

After the longest awkward silence I've ever sat through, Principal Davis said everyone was allowed to hang out in the gym until school was out, and encouraged the candidates to mingle with the crowd.

I know it sounds crazy for an election, but because Principal Davis wanted a new president in less than a week, he thought doing an extreme "meet and greet" session was necessary so students could really get to know who they were voting for.

"Chase!" Zoe said, running over to me. "How'd you like my speech?"

I hesitated. "I, uh, actually didn't hear any of it. I had to step out for a second, but I bet I would've loved it if I *was* here."

"Thanks?" Zoe said, making it sound like a question. "You should've been here. You're my campaign manager! What if I needed you during the speech?"

I wanted to argue, but I knew she was right. "I'm sorry. It won't happen again."

"Better not," she joked.

Gavin joined us, taking Zoe's hand into his. "Awesome speech!"

"Thanks!" Zoe said. "You don't think I sounded shaky, do you? I was super nervous."

"Not at all!" Gavin said. "If you were nervous, you didn't show it. You were well spoken, and very straightforward. Really, it was great."

Zoe blushed.

I scanned the gym full of sixth graders, looking for Naomi. The crowd of students was so thick that I couldn't see anything beyond ten feet. Most of the kids were clumped into groups around the other candidates. Even Zoe was attracting a horde of students. In another few minutes, she would have to start answering individual questions and addressing the students who are interested in voting for her.

"Do either of you see Naomi?" I asked my cousin and Gavin.

Gavin shook his head, standing on his tiptoes and gazing over the heads of sixth graders.

"Not since before the assembly," Zoe said. "Is something wrong?"

I tightened my lips. Zoe knew Naomi had a crush on me, since it was *her* note the Scavengers took, but I couldn't say anything. "No, nothing's wrong. I was just wondering where she went."

At that moment, the speaker system cackled overhead. There was a brief pause as the announcer fumbled with the microphone. And then, a boy's voice spoke. It was the same boy who had addressed Naomi and me in the dungeon. "Attention, please! May I have your attention!" the bubbly voice said. "Sixth grader Chase Cooper is currently struggling with fulfilling his

40

destiny! We encourage you to high-five him every time you see him to give him the guts to continue! Don't forget to ask him about it too! Talking about it helps, Chase!"

My jaw dropped. What in the world was that announcement all about? How did the Scavengers think *that* was going to encourage me to join their club?

The students gathered around Zoe started turning toward me. Then came the questions.

"Chase, what's up? What're you struggling with?"

"Yeah, man. Whatever it is, you know you can talk to me."

"Go for it, man! Whatever that dude was talking about, you should just dive right in. Do it!"

"What kind of destiny are you supposed to fulfill? What were they talking about?"

"Tell us, Chase, what's going on? Seriously, if you need to cry, my shoulder's here for you, okay?"

Oh. *That* was the purpose of the announcement – unwanted attention. And way *too much* unwanted attention, to the point where I was shaking my head and telling everyone I had no idea what it was about.

But that only fueled their questions. Students pushed the issue harder, trying to get me to fess up to something I couldn't talk about.

"Chase, come on, man. Don't say it's nothing. What's up?"

"Bro, you can tell me! We're all sailing in this ocean we call life. Now and then some of us find ourselves overboard. Bro, tell—bro, tell me—bro, look at me, bro. Let me throw you a life saver."

If the Scavengers wanted to put pressure on me, they were definitely off to a good start.

Tuesday. 7:35 AM. Outside the front doors of Buchanan.

The next morning, I made it to school at a decent time, *before* the first bell rang. I was early enough that I had plenty of time to swing by the cafeteria to get a sausage biscuit and a juice.

Kids were still randomly asking me if something was going on, but it wasn't as bad as it was after the assembly. Most of the students would just point at me in the hallway and say something nice, which probably would've felt great if I knew it wasn't because of a fake announcement.

As I was sitting at one of the tables, Zoe took the seat across from me. My cousin was always early to school. *Always.* She was on the volleyball team, which had practice at six in the A.M. *But wait, there's more!* Practice ended at seven, so Zoe joined the debate team to fill the rest of that time before school started.

"Yo," Zoe said, setting a bottled juice on the table.

"Morning," I said with a mouth full of sausage biscuit.

"So are you going to tell me what that announcement was about yesterday or what?" Zoe said, spinning the cap off her drink.

I remembered the Scavengers warning. I wasn't too keen on learning what they meant by my *"complete and utter destruction,"* so decided to keep it from Zoe.

"No idea," I said, taking another huge chomp from my biscuit so I wouldn't have to talk anymore.

"Was it a prank?" Zoe asked. "I bet Wyatt was behind it. Did you hear his speech yesterday?"

I nodded, pushing dry biscuit around my mouth with my

tongue.

"The nerve of him! Saying all that stuff about our moose mascot!"

"Weren't you unhappy with that too though?"

Zoe stuttered. "Well, I mean, yeah, but *I* can say it. I'm your cousin so I'm supposed to give you hard time. I never actually felt hatred toward it."

"A lot of kids do," I said.

"Chase!" someone yelled from across the room.

I turned, expecting them to say something about another shoulder to cry on.

"Congrats, man!" the boy shouted, tossing me a thumbs-up gesture. "Glad to see you got your destiny thing figured out! Good luck!"

I stared, dumbfounded about what the boy was talking about.

He continued. "Your posters are everywhere out here! You've got my vote for sure, good buddy!"

Zoe's eyes slowly met mine. "Um, cousin, *what's* he talking about?"

My eye twitched. I didn't know for sure, but I had my suspicions. My terrible *terrible* suspicions.

Tuesday. 7:40 AM. The lobby.

Zoe and I stared at the poster in the hallway. The same poster was plastered all the way down the hall as far as the eye could see. On the huge poster was my school photo. Someone had added the school flag waving in the background and an eagle soaring under me. At the top of the poster was a circle with the words, "CHASE COOPER FOR PRESIDENT. IF VOTING FOR CHASE IS WRONG, YOU DON'T WANT TO BE RIGHT."

Zoe pushed her lips to the side. "Sooooo, this is new."

I said nothing. The Scavengers were behind the posters; I had no doubt about that. If I said anything to Zoe, it could mean disaster for me, or worse, for her.

My cousin looked at me. "What is this?"

Again, I said nothing. I wanted so bad to tell her everything, but I couldn't bring myself to do it. Fear makes you do stupid things sometimes.

"You could've told me you were gonna run, you know!" Zoe said. "I would've been fine with it!"

Poomph!

"Perfect!" Melvin, the reporter, said. He was standing a short distance behind my cousin and me, camera in hand, under a ball of smoke that erupted when the flashbulb went off. "I think I really caught the anger in that one! Can I have another shot of you two fighting? After that, we can do a good handshake one. No, y'know what? Nevermind. Let's get more fighting! Kids eat that up!"

"Get lost, Melvin," Zoe growled. She turned back to me. "And you! I feel like you stabbed me in the back!"

"But I--" I started to say, but stopped.

"But what?" Zoe said. "*What?*"

I sighed. Saying nothing only made me look *more* guilty. *Poomph!*

"Nice," Melvin whispered.

"Quit taking pictures!" I cried.

"You know you can't be my campaign manager now, right?" Zoe asked, raising her voice. She was clearly upset, and the students gathering around us could totally tell. "So now I'm left with no campaign manager, and only *four* days left until the election. I'm glad *you* got *your* posters out, but that means I'll be scrambling to catch up!"

My mouth opened slightly. "Zoe, I..."

"Thanks," Zoe said as she stormed off. "Thanks for

nothing!"

"Bummer," said a student nearby. "Don't let it get to you though. You got *my* vote."

"And *mine*," said another student.

"Mine too!" yet another student said.

"And *my* axe!" some weird dude proclaimed from somewhere I couldn't see. "Which means I'll be voting for you!"

In that moment, I felt really weird. I was torn. On the one hand, Zoe was disappointed in me. But on the other hand, several students just told me they'd vote for me. I was sad yet flattered at the same time.

Daisy, one of the other presidential candidates pushed through the crowd. She extended her open hand to me. "May the best kid win," she said with a smile.

As I shook her hand, Melvin snapped another photograph. That kid was starting to get on my nerves.

"What made you decide to run?" Daisy asked, still shaking

my hand like she was in a job interview.

"I just, uh…" I said. "I dunno. I just wanted to?"

Daisy arched an eyebrow. "Is that a question?"

I shook my head, trying to think of something better. "I just thought the race could use a fifth student."

"Ah," Daisy said. "Well, anyways, I'm glad to run alongside you. Good luck."

"Right," I grumbled. "You too."

Tuesday. 7:45 AM. Homeroom.

I was the last in homeroom, on purpose I might add because Zoe was supposed to be in there too.

Supposed to be.

I took my same spot as usual at the back of class. My cousin usually sat in front of me, but she wasn't in the room. It wasn't like her to be *late* for anything, which meant she probably wasn't even going to come to homeroom at all. Being the super straight-A student she was, it was likely she was in the library.

Brayden was next to me. He leaned over and spoke quietly. "I saw your posters," he said. "Pretty cool."

I was surprised. "You're not upset about it?"

"Not at all!" he replied. "You're my best friend! Why would I be upset about that?"

I shrugged my shoulders.

"Listen, man," Brayden said. "This whole week, we have to agree to not get upset with each other, alright? No matter what happens, this election is just a stupid election, but it's not as important as our friendship, got it?"

I smiled, and we bumped fists. Brayden was someone I could trust, and I wanted to tell him that it wasn't my choice to run for president, and that it was the Scavengers who were messing with me, but I couldn't. Not yet at least. Brayden doesn't even know the Scavengers exist, and that wasn't a bubble of his I wanted to burst.

More realistically though – the posters were just a prank to bring more unwanted attention to me. There was no way my name was *actually* on the ballot. I was willing to bet if I just ignored the whole thing, everything would blow over, and the real election wouldn't even be affected. Basically I wasn't going to play the game with the Scavengers. My posters might be in the hallway, but that didn't mean I had to run.

Mrs. Robinson stood from her desk and started with the announcements. "Good morning, students. First things first, I suppose. You all know the election for Buchanan's new president is going to be held this Friday, right *before* lunch. Votes will be counted *during* lunch, and the new president will be announced at the assembly *after* lunch. Aaaaaand," Mrs. Robinson trailed off. "It looks like we have another student running now. Chase Cooper?"

Not good.

Everyone in class turned in their seat to look at me. Don't you hate it when they do that?

Mrs. Robinson's eyebrows lifted. "Nice," she added, and then droned on with the rest of the announcements. Her voice became a muffled trumpet in my head as my world crumbled.

The game the Scavengers were playing seemed to be for keeps. The posters with my ugly mug were hanging all over the school, and apparently they were legit. I *was* running for class president now, whether I liked it or not.

Tuesday. 8:30 AM. Art class.

When I got to art class, I was happy to see Zoe in her seat. Homeroom was a period she could skip easily, but art wasn't so much.

I wasn't planning on letting the Scavengers get the best of me. I was going to withdraw my name from the ballot, but patching things up with Zoe came first.

I set my book bag on the floor and sat at my desk next to hers. "Look, about all the posters," I started.

Zoe interrupted me. "S'cool," she said, smiling softly. It was genuine, but there was still a hint of sadness to it. "I was just shocked. That's all."

"Really?" I asked. "You don't hate me for it?"

Zoe shook her head, making an "are you serious?" face. "I'd never hate you for something like that. I might be disappointed, but just 'cause we won't be working together."

"Don't worry about that," I said without thinking. "By the end of the day, things will be normal again."

Zoe paused, confused. "What do you mean by that?"

I shook my head, making some weird sounds that kind of sounded like I didn't know how to speak. High-pitched grunts mostly. I said too much, and my brain was starting to panic.

"This is about the announcement yesterday, isn't it?" Zoe asked.

Complete and utter destruction.

"It's nothing," I said. "I just meant that since you're not

mad at me, we're good. Things are normal between us, right?"

Again, Zoe paused. She nodded slowly. "Riiiiiight."

The rest of art went on as if everything were normal once again. I was glad because my cousin is the best at giving someone the silent treatment, and since our desks were literally half an inch away from each other, class would've been super awkward.

As students worked on their projects, I was planning my next move with the Scavengers. I decided that I would pay them another visit right before lunch. That way, I wouldn't have to race the bell to get to any classes, plus Naomi could come with.

I'd have to find her before that though – she was probably still embarrassed from the day before, but I wouldn't want to go into the dungeon without her.

Tuesday. 11:25 AM. Before lunch.

"Hi," I said to Naomi when I saw her. I had been standing by her locker, waiting for her.

"Hey," Naomi said softly. Yeah, it was obvious that she was uncomfortable.

"Look," I said. "Please don't let yesterday make things weird between us."

Naomi looked up, finally making eye contact with me. She looked angry. "You think that's *all* that's bothering me?"

"Yeah," I said, unsure. "Up until you said *that*."

"Until yesterday, I thought I knew everything there was to know about this school," Naomi explained. "There weren't any secrets about Buchanan that I didn't know about, and I was proud of it. I knew about our ninja clan. I knew about Wyatt's ninja clan. I knew about Glitch. I even knew about Suckerpunch!"

I felt more confused than ever. "Glitch? Suckerpunch? Naomi, what the *spew* are you talking about?"

She ignored my question. "I knew all the rumors behind the Scavengers, but I also knew there was *no way* they could exist without *me* knowing about them. And since I *didn't* know about them, they couldn't possibly exist, right?"

I stared at Naomi. At least she wasn't being awkward because I knew she had a crush on me.

"Wrong!" she said. "The Scavengers are real, and they're *terrifying!* They're *worse* than I thought! They know my secrets – *our* secrets – *everyone's* secrets! They know things they're not supposed to know! I want nothing to do with them, not now, not ever!"

"Mmmm," I hummed. "Then you're going hate me in about a second."

Naomi stopped, her eyes piercing me. "You're going down there again, aren't you?"

"I have no choice," I said. "You've seen my posters around the school, haven't you?"

She nodded.

"They've waged war on me," I said. "It's not something I want to do, so I need to meet with them. Hopefully I can talk some sense into their leader."

"Do you *know* who their leader is? Naomi asked.

I thought for a second. "No. I have no idea. It's probably the tall kid who spoke the most."

"I doubt they can be reasoned with," Naomi said. "I was there yesterday. They didn't seem interested in leaving you alone."

I sighed. "I know, but I have to try. Would you come with me?"

Naomi didn't answer.

So I tried to be cute. "Pleeeeeease? With strawberry syrup, whipped cream, and cinnamon glazed pecans on top?"

At that, Naomi laughed. "What's with you and sweets? I bet your dentist makes millions off you."

"Not me," I joked. "My *parents*."

"Fine," Naomi said. "But under one condition."

"Name it."

"Never speak about my crush on you," Naomi said. "That was *months* ago. I'm totes over it now, got it?"

I had to force myself to keep a straight face. "Got it."

Tuesday. 11:40 AM. The dungeon.

When Naomi and I reached the hallway with room 001, I stopped to get my thoughts together.

Naomi was in the middle of sentence. "...which is why I feel like the Scavengers are kind of like the ninjas to actual ninjas. Y'know what I mean? Like, they were so secret that not even a ninja clan knew about them! Like, while ninjas live in the shadows, the Scavengers live in the *ninja's* shadow. Messed up, right?"

I watched the hallway for any movement, making sure we were alone. I didn't want to admit it, but I was scared. I could tell Naomi was trying to lighten the mood.

"Chase?" Naomi said, stepping in front of me. "Earth to Chase. You're needed back on Earth, sir. Hey, here's one – if a ninja falls in the forest, and nobody is around to hear it, did the ninja make a sound?"

Smiling, I answered. "For starters, ninjas *don't* fall. For um, *seconders*, the ninja wouldn't make a sound anyway – he's a *ninja*. And thirdly, just trust me on it, if the ninja *did* make a sound then he was *never* a ninja to begin with."

"Take *that* imaginary ninja who fell in the forest," Naomi said. "Burn, sucka!"

Putting my game-face on, I tightened my lips. "I'm just going to tell them to knock it off."

"Because *that* worked yesterday," Naomi said sarcastically.

"I'll just say I'll go straight the principal if they don't quit."

Naomi made a "*duh*" face. "You probably should've done that first."

"You might be right, but I'm afraid I'll just make things worse if I do that first. I at least want to give them a chance to do the right thing."

"Some kids don't *want* to do the right thing," Naomi said. "Some kids just want to play dumb games. You heard them yesterday! They control everything in the school! What makes you think they'll stop playing *that* game?"

"You're not helping," I said, starting my march to room 001.

Naomi followed me, continuing her case. "Seriously, I don't think this is something you should even flirt with anymore. It's blazingly obvious that these kids are hardcore."

"So I should just ignore it? Pretend it's not happening?" I asked, stopping in front of the spot we stopped at the day before. The broken water fountain behind us was still pumping water through its spigot.

"No," Naomi said. "I don't know the answer to that."

"Exactly," I said. "So this is why I'm going to try this first. I promise, if it doesn't work, I'll do it your way."

I turned and reached for the handle of the door to room 001...

But the door wasn't there. Neither were the fake vines.

"Ummmm," I hummed, glancing down both sides of the hall. "Isn't this where we were yesterday?"

"There's the busted water fountain," Naomi said, pointing. "And the room down there is 002."

Where a door should've been, stood a massive brick wall with a weird street sign on it that had an arrow pointing to the left along with the words "Brackenbury Lane" on it. "What?" I asked, confused.

Naomi knocked on the bricks to check if they were fake, but they weren't. She even hurt her hand on them. "If there was ever a time to freak out, it would be now," she said, rubbing her sore knuckles.

I reached out my closed hand to knock on the wall, but Naomi stopped me before I could.

"It's solid," she said, waving the pain out of her hand. "I

wouldn't bother."

I sighed, but listened. It wasn't necessary to bang on the bricks if it was just going to hurt my hand. I *need* my hands!

A rustling came from down the hall, and then a petite voice spoke. "You guys okay?"

It was Daisy.

I pointed at the brick wall, where room 001 was supposed to be. "There should be a door here, right? Are we crazy?"

Daisy stepped up to the bricks, running her fingers down the wall. Her eyes squinted like she was thinking. "I'm not sure," she said. "If there was, I never had class in it, but now that you say it... I *think* I remember a door being here. Weird." She turned around and changed the subject. "So how's the race going?"

"It's going," I replied.

"What'd you think of my speech yesterday?" Daisy asked, obviously fishing for compliments.

I hesitated, but decided that honesty was best. "I missed it. I had to step out of the gym for a few minutes."

"Oh," Daisy said sadly. "Oh well. It's not like I would've won your vote since you're running." She turned and headed toward the stairs that led to the ground floor. "See ya guys upstairs."

"See ya," Naomi grumbled, returning her attention to the magical brick wall.

Room 001 wasn't there anymore, even though Naomi and I had *just* been inside it the day before. I knew we were in the right spot because the broken water fountain was right behind us. There was no way someone could've built a *brick wall* in less than a day! Not without at least a *bit* of construction dust in the hallway, but the floors were clean!

A chill traveled down my spine, shooting into my legs until my toes tickled.

"Let's get out of here," I said, looking over my shoulder. "This is too weird, even for *me*."

Naomi nodded, and together, we went back to the ground level of Buchanan School. Lunch had just started, and being around a whole bunch of kids sounded better than standing in the cold dungeon.

Tuesday. 11:45 AM. The lobby.

I was still trying to wrap my head around how room 001 could've disappeared when Naomi and I entered the lobby.

"That's not even possible," Naomi said. "That door *has* to be there. It just *has* to. I bet it was behind those bricks."

I was only half-listening when I answered. "Yeah, but being down there gave me the creeps…" I stopped, watching the *huge* line of students waiting to get into the cafeteria. "What's going on?"

Naomi peered through the tinted glass windows into the lunchroom. "Oh, it looks like a pizza party!"

I slapped my forehead. "That's right! Zoe's party is going—"

But before I could finish my sentence, my cousin screamed at me. "*How could you?*"

I turned to see an irate Zoe, storming across the lobby. Her eyes were red with fire, and her cheeks were wet from… tears?

"What are you—" Again, my cousin interrupted me, but not with sentence. She smacked my face with the soft palm of her hand.

Naomi froze, her eyes wide-opened.

The clap echoed across the lobby, and maybe even across the county. I bet somewhere a flock of birds got scared out of a tree because of that slap. Everyone waiting in line flinched at the same time when they saw it.

"*Oh snap!*"

"I think you mean, oh SLAP!"
"Dang! That girl can hit!"
"Owned!"
I rubbed my cheek. *"What gives? Are you crazy?"*

"That pizza party was for *my* campaign! *I'm* the one who paid for it! What else are you gonna steal of mine?" Zoe screamed.

"What are you talking about? I *just* walked out here!" I replied, but right as I did, I saw what Zoe was talking about.

Through the tinted glasses windows, I saw a banner with my face on it. I took a step closer to the window, still rubbing my burning cheek. And then I read the banner aloud, "Have a slice on me, Chase Cooper. A vote for me means free pizza for you…"

Poomph!

I was beginning the hate the sound of Melvin's camera.

"Zoe, I didn't do this," I said to my cousin, but when I turned around she was gone. I don't know why, but I suddenly felt

60

enraged that Zoe had slapped me in front of everyone only to disappear a second later. "Fine!" I shouted loud enough that she could hear me wherever she was. "Then you can't use my awesome leadership quote!"

I know. I regretted it the second I said it, but everyone was staring at me. I had to save face, right?

Naomi tightened her lips, but didn't say anything. She looked at me, and then looked down the hallway, to where Zoe had run off.

Pushing my foot into the carpet, I took off running. I barely made it a few steps before a taller boy got in my way. With his chest pushed out, he bumped into me. I staggered a bit, but managed to keep myself standing.

"Move!" I ordered.

The boy refused, smirking the entire time. He raised his hand, showing me an index card that had writing on it. "Read it," he said.

I stared at the card, confused. "Huh?"

"Read it," the boy said, "Or we'll tell everyone you're a ninja."

Grinding my teeth, I looked at the card again. If all I had to do was read a sentence to avoid having my secret exposed, then fine. I read the card aloud. "My name is Chase Cooper, and I approve this message."

The smirk never left the boy's face.

"What's this about?" I asked. "Why'd you make me read that?"

Quietly, the boy spoke, ignoring my question. "We are everywhere…"

"And nowhere," a girl said, stepping out to my side.

"Everything you believe to be secret…"

"…is not. We know everything about everyone."

Scavengers. And they were finishing each other's sentence, which was more eerie than you'd think. Both the boy and the girl weren't students I recognized, but in a school as large as Buchanan, I wasn't surprised.

Naomi took the spot on my other side, opposite of the female Scavenger. I looked for Melvin, but he wasn't around anymore. The line of students for pizza started moving quickly enough that nobody was paying attention to us.

The boy's eyes narrowed. "You've offended us, and now you must pay."

I put my hands out in front of me, ready to block any punches that were thrown.

The girl giggled. "Not with a fight," she said. "We will destroy you for rejecting our invitation, but not with bruises or black eyes…"

"It's your *legacy* we're after," the boy said.

After that, both of the Scavengers disappeared through the cafeteria doors.

As if on cue, Wyatt and Olivia stepped *out* of the doors to the lunchroom.

"Geez, really?" Naomi whispered to me. "It's like all your enemies are lining up to take shots at you."

I imagined a conference room filled with all the kids that have tried messing with me over the past few months. They were seated at a huge table made from mahogany, sharing stories of how they *almost* got me "that one time." They'd probably even have a sign made for the name of their evil league, something along the lines of "Chase Haters Club." There'd be a yearly fee of $99 that had to be – y'know what? Let's get back to the story…

His mouth wet with pizza grease, Wyatt held up a paper plate with *three* fat slices of pepperoni pizza on it. "Nice move with the pizza," he said. "But it won't win you the election."

Olive had her own plate with several slices of pizza stacked on top of each other. "My boo's got this election in the palm of his hands! He's only a few points behind you, but by the end of the week, he'll be in the lead."

"A few points behind me?" I asked. "How do you know how many points anyone has?"

"Student surveys," Melvin said as he walked toward us. He had his own plate of pizza, which must've been why he disappeared earlier. "Chase, right now you're taking the lead."

"I am?" I asked, not surprised since everyone thought I had given them free pizza.

"Daisy's in second, Zoe's in the third, Brayden's in fourth, and Wyatt?" Melvin said, glancing at the leader of the red ninjas. "You're in last."

"So much for being a few points behind me," I added.

Wyatt tore a chunk of pizza off into his mouth. "We'll see what place you're in by the end of the week."

"How's *Daisy* in second place?" Olive asked.

"Homeschooled kids," Melvin said. "Seems most of them are leaning on her side."

"Homeschooled kids shouldn't count!" Wyatt huffed. "They're not students here!"

"They count," Melvin said flatly. "One of my best friends is homeschooled and lives in the Buchanan district. Personally, I'm *glad* he's got a vote if it means you've got less of a chance of becoming president."

Wyatt let out a "pft" sound as he made an ugly face, but he didn't say another word.

Olive stuck out her tongue as the creepy couple went back into the lunchroom to stuff their faces with more greasy pizza.

Naomi said goodbye and then stood in line behind the other

students waiting for lunch.

It was just Melvin and me in the lobby after a few moments.

The reporter sighed, holding his oversized camera in front of him. "Looks like you're the kid to follow around, right?"

"Because I'm winning?"

"Nope," Melvin said. "I got a text message from an unknown number telling me I should tag along with you at all times."

"Why?"

Melvin paused. "It said you know something about the ninjas in the school."

I choked, coughing loudly.

Putting his hand on my shoulder, Melvin said, "You alright? Need some water?"

Hacking violently, I put my hand to my mouth, shaking my head.

"Between you and me?" Melvin started. "I *know* there are ninjas hiding in the school. In fact, do you remember that ninja act in the talent show a couple weeks back?"

"Yeah," I said, avoiding eye contact.

"Well, I believe that *wasn't* an act," Melvin said. "I think those ninjas were in the middle of a battle that just happened to land in front of an audience. If I can bring this story to the light of day, you know how much attention it would muster up? It'd be the biggest news to hit Buchanan since the *Chocolate Milk Disaster of 2001*."

"The what?"

"Students are limited to two chocolate milk boxes during lunch for a reason. Back in 2001, that limit was lifted, and students were allowed to drink as much as they could afford," Melvin explained. "Kids were barfing chocolate milk in record numbers. You know how some kids give no warning that they're going to puke? Instead, they just pop at their desk? Just think of an entire student body doing that. All. Day. Long."

I gagged. "Can you imagine the smell?"

"I'd rather not," Melvin said. "This ninja story is going to blow that one out of the water. I'll be the most famous kid reporter in the world."

There was no doubt in my mind that it was the Scavengers

64

who sent Melvin the text. If Melvin trailed me long enough, he was sure to find out about my secret ninja clan.

Running for president. Damaging my friendship with Zoe. Making things awkward between Naomi and me. Telling Melvin that I knew anything about the ninjas. All that, and it was *only* Tuesday!

I didn't even *think* about what else could possibly go wrong, because the truth was I knew things *could* be worse... I just didn't realize how *much* worse it was about to get.

Wednesday. 7:39 AM. Homeroom.

When I got to school the next morning, I had a sick feeling in the pit of my stomach, like something terrible was waiting for me as soon as I stepped through the doors. I was surprised to see that it was just the opposite.

Normally I can make it to homeroom without a single person noticing me. My run for president changed that.

"*Chaaaaaaaase!*" said a boy wearing circle sunglasses as he pointed at me with both his hands.

A girl smiled at me, touching my shoulder as she walked by me in the hallway. "Awesome pizza party yesterday! Me and all my friends are *totes magotes* voting for you!"

Someone shouted from down the hall. "*Chase Cooper! The Coopster for president!*"

Everyone in the corridor cheered.

And to be completely honest – I didn't *hate* all the attention I was getting.

For those first few comments, I tried to maintain an air of integrity, keeping my head high while filtering through the crowd, but the crowd grew thicker. Soon it was impossible for me to even move because of the wall of students around me. I couldn't help but smile.

"Chase, can I get your autograph?" asked a girl, holding her diary out for me to see. The book was opened to a page where she drew a heart around my name.

Another boy pushed forward. "Dude, street hockey tonight!

My street! Everyone who's cool is gonna be there! No need to bring skates 'cause we'll have a pair for you!"

Someone else held a baby doll to my face. "Kiss my baby, Chase!"

"Guys, guys, guys!" I said, patting at the air in front of me. I was going to be serious, but my ego got the best of me. Can you blame me? "Easy on the Coopster! There's plenty of me to go around!"

Everyone laughed.

Wednesday. 7:50 AM. Homeroom.

I spent so much time joking with my new fans in the hallway that I didn't even hear the second bell ring. Principal Davis had to break the crowd apart, but nobody was in trouble. He always threatens detention, but never delivers on it.

Mrs. Robinson was already in the middle of the morning announcements when I entered the room. A couple boys nodded at me when I walked in. A few girls fluttered their eyelashes in my direction.

Being popular was something I could get used to.

"S'up, King Tut?" I said, sitting in the desk behind my cousin. Maybe throwing out random nicknames was a little bigheaded of me.

She didn't answer.

I leaned forward in my chair. "Hello?"

Again, Zoe said nothing. She was still mad, and she was showing me by giving me the silent treatment. Even after my awesome morning, I still felt bad that she was upset. And she had every right to be! The pizza party that was supposed to be hers was hijacked by the Scavengers, turning it into mine!

"Zoe," I whispered. "I'm sorry about yesterday."

"Then why did you do it?" Zoe replied swiftly.

For a split second, I thought about unloading all my garbage about the Scavengers and their role in how my week was turning out, but again, I decided to keep it to myself. There wasn't any reason to involve my cousin yet since the fire was still burning.

68

"I can't tell you what's going on," I said, "but I'm going to fix this. I promise."

Zoe folded her arms. I watched the back of her head as she replied. "This isn't something you can fix, Chase. You've done too much damage this time."

"But…" I said, trailing off. I didn't know what else to say.

For the rest of homeroom, I sat quietly trying to figure out what my next move against the Scavengers was going to be. If I let it go on for too much longer, I was going to lose Zoe as a friend, and her friendship meant more to me than anything.

Wednesday. 11:30 AM. Lunch.

The rest of the morning proved to be awkward since I have several classes with Zoe. The silent treatment she was giving me was like an invisible wall separating us. It was even worse because in *all* of our classes, our seats were right next to each other. Her refusal to even *look* at me was driving me crazy.

During lunch, I was able to take my mind off her for at least a few minutes after I sat at a table alone with my food.

Just then, Jake slammed his tray on the table and sat across from me. His wolf pack remained standing, scouring the room with their beady eyes.

"Where's Melvin?" Jake asked.

I grunted. "Huh? Who? The reporter?"

Jake pushed his tongue around like he was trying to get food out of his teeth. "Yes, the *reporter*."

"Why?"

"Because I'm *looking* for him. That's why," Jake answered, irritated.

"I don't know," I replied. "I haven't seen him today. What do you need him for?"

Jake smacked his lips, and then spit a tiny piece of food onto the floor. I guess he got it out of his teeth. Standing from the table, he spoke. "If you see him, don't tell him I'm looking for him. In fact, if you see him, come find me."

"What makes you think I'm gonna do that?" I asked.

Jake looked me dead in the eye. "Because we both want him

to keep his mouth shut about ninjas."

Great, I thought. More drama for me to swim around in. Somehow Jake knew Melvin wanted to write an article about the secret ninjas at school.

After Jake left, I hardly touched my food. I was too busy watching everyone in the lunchroom. Naomi was eating with some of her friends. Zoe was making rounds, going from table to table, talking politics and trying to win some votes. Daisy, Brayden, and Wyatt were doing the same thing at different spots in the cafeteria. If I were actually running for president, I'd probably do the same.

Right then, I heard Melvin's voice, but I couldn't see him. "I *knew* following you was the right thing to do! Felt it in my gut!"

Slowly, I looked all around me, but couldn't see Melvin anywhere. "Um," I said. "Where are you?"

"Down here!" Melvin whispered from *under* the table.

"Okaaaay?" I said, not making any sudden movements. And then I realized he *had* to have heard my conversation with Jake.

"Tell me what you know about the ninjas!" Melvin ordered, still whispering as he pressed a pencil against the paper of a small notebook.

"Dude-man," I said. "Get outta there."

"Tell me what I want to know!" Melvin said. "*Why* did Jake confront you about ninjas? *What* do you know about them?"

I kicked at the reporter, not hard, but just enough to annoy him, like he was a bug I was trying to shoo away. "Get *out* from there!"

Melvin scooted out from under the table. The back of his shirt was caked in crumbs and dried gravy. It was gross.

"What'll it take for you to talk?" Melvin asked. "Huh? Name it! Anything! I swear I won't mention your name in the article."

"Get lost," I said. "Jake's looking for you, and if you stand around here for too long, he'll *find* you. And that's something you definitely *don't* want."

Melvin looked over his shoulder, tapping his pencil on his notepad. "There's a story here," he said. "And I can either take it from you or you can give it to me."

I paused, acting like I was going to say something important. "Alright, this one time," I started.

"Mmm?" Melvin hummed with a smile, scratching words into his notebook.

"I thought I found a human finger half buried in the dirt out on the track," I said. "But it turned out to be just a dried up hot dog."

The reporter's pencil stopped. "Funny," he stated sarcastically.

"Seriously!" I said. "Sounds like a happy ending, but where'd the hot dog come from, Melvin? Huh? *Where did the hot dog come from?*"

"So immature," Melvin said with a drop of disgust in his voice.

"Me? Immature?" I asked. "I collect comic books because they're going to be worth something someday, okay? I'm investing in my future! Does that sound like something an *immature* person would do?"

Melvin shook his head, but not like he was agreeing with

me. It was more like he was disappointed that I wasn't helping him with his ninja story.

I sighed, turning back to my food. "Whatever, dude. Just leave me alone."

Melvin paused like he was going to say something, but he didn't. Suddenly he spun around and jogged toward the cafeteria doors.

"C'mon," I heard Jake's voice say from nearby. "He just saw us."

I gritted my teeth, frustrated because I knew Jake had spotted Melvin. I couldn't just sit by, knowing that Jake was planning on giving the reporter the beat-down of the century.

Jake was storming down the aisle. Right before he crossed my path again, I grabbed my tray of food and jumped up from the table.

The leader of the wolf pack slammed into me. I could've kept my balance, but I needed to make a scene if Jake was going to be stopped.

Flipping my tray toward me, I splashed all the nasty cafeteria food all over my face and hair. Sloppy Joes and banana cream pie are *not* two items I'd recommend going up your nose.

"Dude!" I shouted, acting shocked.

The students in the cafeteria snapped their attention toward me like squirrels when they hear twigs snap.

Jake took a step back with his arms out, looking down at the mess of food on his shirt. "*Are you serious?*"

I stole a glance behind me, trying to see if Melvin was still around. He wasn't, which meant he was safe... for the time being.

I started acting upset so Jake would waste more time arguing with me rather than searching for Melvin. Pointing at my crushed apple on the floor, I said, "No, are *you* serious? You just *killed* my apple, dude! You think those things just grow on trees?"

Jake started to argue, but his face froze. I could almost see his brain crashing. "Uh... yeah?"

I threw my arms up. "Oh right, like there's some kind of *magical* tree out there that just *grows* apples on its branches! Some sort of mystical all-powerful *tree* that some wizard created *just* to show his big brother that he was all grown up now, right?"

Jake's eye's narrowed as his jaw dropped a little more. "*What* are you talking about?"

"Sorry," I said, smearing greasy beef off my face. "I just *really* wanted that apple."

Jake took one step toward me and growled. "I know you did that to keep Melvin safe, but you can't be there all the time. I *will* find him, and I *will* keep him from writing that article."

I acted clueless. "What? Was Melvin around? Where?"

Jake's jaw muscles twitched, but the conversation ended there. He raised his fist, the signal for his wolf pack to follow him. Like mindless animals, they trailed behind him as he returned to one of the lunch tables.

Wiping the rest of the slop off my face, I took a knee and started scooping food back onto my tray. After all the junk I'd been through in the week, I felt a little better at having helped Melvin avoid a black eye or two.

That moment only lasted for a second though.

The lights in the cafeteria dimmed. Hushed whispers floated through the crowd in anticipation for whatever was happening.

At the front of the cafeteria, the stage curtains swept open, revealing a giant LCD television sitting alone. An image of Buchanan School slowly came to life onscreen as the audio played through the cafeteria speaker system.

"Buchanan School…" said the narrator's voice. "A place of peace, hope, and love. A place where friendships are melded in the fires of life. A place where education is the highest priority… right after pizza parties."

The kids in the lunchroom laughed simultaneously.

The video went on, filtering through photos of students in class. "But there is another threat to our well-being…"

I gazed at the television, hypnotized by the video.

The image on the screen turned bright red as Brayden's class photo spun to a stop at the center. "This boy, who you know as Brayden, has a dark secret."

Gulping, I shot my eyes around the room looking for my best friend. Finally, I found him standing at the far corner of the cafeteria. His brow was furrowed, and his lips were tightly pressed against his teeth as he watched the video.

"Brayden is a self-proclaimed werewolf hunter," the narrator said calmly. "He's devoted most of his life to finding and capturing a real-life werewolf, which any sane person can tell you – they don't exist. Brayden is chasing ghost stories."

The screen flashed white as a "*JUN!*" sound effect cut through the cafeteria. There was another photo of Brayden on the screen – a much more *embarrassing* photo. It was one where he was wearing his werewolf hunting armor.

"Is *this* the student you want running the school?" the narrator asked.

Holy wow. Who on Earth had the guts to play a commercial like that in front of the entire school? Who would even sink to the level of making a smear campaign video?

Brayden's red photo faded out on the screen, only to be replaced by a bright and shiny photo of…

Me.

All I could do was gawk at the commercial.

The narrator continued. "A vote for Chase Cooper means a vote for reality. Chase lives in the *real* world, with *real* kids, and has *real* goals. A vote for Chase Cooper means no time wasted on the pursuit of fake monsters. A vote for Chase Cooper… is a vote for the future."

The commercial faded to black, but before it completely disappeared, my voice came through the speaker system. "*My name is Chase Cooper, and I approve this message.*"

I bit my tongue. The Scavenger recorded me when I read that stupid index card! Why did I even read that thing? Why can't my brain put these things together *before* bad things happen?

Principal Davis jumped onto the stage and shut the television off, but it was too late. The message had been played.

The lights returned in the cafeteria, but the students remained mostly quiet. More whispers came from the crowd, but the conversation wasn't about me. It was about Brayden and his monster obsession.

When I turned to look at my best friend, he was glaring at me, fuming. He was so angry that I could see the muscles twitching in his jaw. I've never seen him so upset.

The principal grabbed my arm, yanking me across the cafeteria. It was sudden, but I was thankful that I had a reason to leave.

Wednesday. 11:45 AM. The principal's office.

"At what point did you think it was okay to make a video like that?" Principal Davis asked loudly, sitting behind his desk with his arms folded.

I didn't answer.

"Do you know the world of trouble you've put Brayden in? Aren't the two of you best friends?"

I nodded.

"So did it never occur to you that playing a smear video like that would maybe hurt your friendship?"

Again, I didn't answer.

"This is nuts, even for *you*," Principal Davis said. "I can't just let this go, Chase." He sighed, slumping down into his leather chair. Leaning back, he folded his hands on his stomach. After a moment, he spoke again. "When you put your name in for president, I was excited. You've been a great addition to this school since day one. You've been nothing but a force of good and an outstanding role model…"

Every word penetrated me. I wanted to cry out and say that I was still those things and that it was the Scavengers who were tarnishing my reputation, but I couldn't bring myself to do it.

"I want to believe there's more to the story than a simple video," Principal Davis said. "Is there *anything* you want to say for yourself?"

"No," I said softly.

Principal Davis nodded as he delivered my punishment. "Detention for the rest of the day today. All-day-detention tomorrow, but you'll serve it by cleaning the school grounds – community service. And on Friday, you'll be on the cleanup crew for the cafeteria after breakfast."

"Okay," I said.

Scribbling on a pad of paper, Principal Davis filled out the paperwork that would probably get filed away in my permanent record. I sat patiently, watching the hands on his clock tick.

All week I had been trying to figure out a way to get out of the way of the Scavengers path of destruction, and Principal Davis just did it for me by making it so I was basically behind bars until the election on Friday.

I exhaled slowly, sinking back in my seat. If I had to sit in detention for a day and half, it would mean that I could just coast through the rest of the week on cruise control.

Crazy, right? Have you ever heard of someone so excited to rot away in detention before? Yeah, me neither.

Wednesday. 1:00 PM. Detention.

Mr. Lien was resting his head on his hand when I entered the room for detention. He was the teacher in charge because he taught the computer class, which was in the room across the hall. Basically, he was the unlucky staff member who was closest to the detention room, making him the most convenient choice.

And you could tell he hated it.

With his eyes half-shut, he mumbled, pointing to a sheet of paper at the edge of his desk. "Name and grade."

I snatched the pen and signed my name. After that, I took the desk at the end of the row, farthest from the door.

"Same routine as every time," Mr. Lien said. "I'll be between this room and my class across the hall. You need anything, just shout at me. Understood?"

"Yessir," I said.

The teacher pushed himself away from his desk and waddled out of the room. Because of the combination of being overweight and short, he moved so weird. It was like he was an alien wearing a human disguise.

Finally alone, I dropped my book bag onto the floor and rolled my head around in large circles, stretching my muscles out so I could relax.

The last time I was in detention, time seemed to practically stop. Every second felt like an hour, and every hour felt like an eternity. I remember being so bored I felt like I was going to explode, but not this time.

79

This time I was glad to be away from everyone else. Away from the noise. Away from the gossip. Away from the election. Away from my friends who hated me. Just... *away.*

I was so *okay* with being alone that I didn't even care about keeping myself busy. I had stacks of assignments I could begin working on, but instead, I folded my arms on the table in front of me and buried my head in them.

"No sleeping in detention!" said a voice from the door.

The sudden sound scared me to death. I jerked to the side, completely sliding off my chair like a bumbling fool. "Great," I sighed, looking at who had frightened me.

It was the reporter. *Melvin.*

Shutting the door behind him, Melvin stepped farther into the room. He chuckled as he held his hand out to me. "Such grace," he said. "I guess I can cross you off the list of people who I suspect are ninjas."

I faked a laugh. "Guess so," I said, taking the boy's hand so he could help me up. "What're you doing in here?"

"I thought you'd like to know that Brayden just dropped out of the election," Melvin said. "Obviously, because of your video."

"It *wasn't* my video," I said, upset. Brayden was really looking forward to running for president. And now, because of me, his whole reputation has a muddy spot on it. My mouth felt dry as I thought about Brayden making the decision to drop out.

"No? Then whose video was it?"

I started to answer, but stopped. Fear of the Scavengers made me hold my tongue.

"That's what I thought." Melvin sat on the chair next to me. "Anyways, I wanted to ask you some questions about the ninja. Figured this was a good time to do it since you can't go anywhere."

I gulped. "Look, dude. I know nothing of what you're talkin' about."

"Yet *you* were the one I was told to follow!"

"By some random text message?" I asked. "How do you know it wasn't some kind of prank? How do you know that wasn't to keep you distracted from something else? Something bigger?"

Melvin's face grew serious. "You've sparked my interest. What '*bigger*' thing might you be referring to?"

I hesitated for a moment, but decided that I just didn't care about keeping them a secret anymore. "*Scavengers.*"

Melvin chocked out a laugh. "Yeah, right! Like the Scavengers even exist!"

I looked at the reporter, surprised. "*Really?* Ninjas are secretly hiding in the halls of Buchanan, but a group of kids who call themselves the Scavengers are a little unbelievable?"

"Ghost stories!" Melvin said arrogantly. "The rumor of the Scavengers only exists to keep kids from unloading their life story in a note to a friend. It's so nobody ever writes anything *overly* personal about themselves or their friends."

"What if I told you," I started, "that the Scavengers are real?"

"I would look you in the eye," Melvin replied. "And say poppycock!"

I laughed. "You're following the wrong story. It's not ninjas you need to worry about. It's the Scavengers. They're real, and they know everything about everyone."

Melvin shook his head, tapping on the desk. "Alright, smart guy. Tell me about the '*Scavengers*,'" he said while making air quotes with his fingers.

Taking a breath, I glanced over my shoulder. I knew we were alone in the room, but I had to double check, just to make sure.

Melvin let a "pft" sound through his nose. It was a short laugh, the kind where I knew he thought I was being dumb.

Finally, I spoke. "You think I'm running in this race on purpose?"

"Yeah," Melvin said flatly without hesitating.

"Well," I paused. "I'm *not. They* put me up to this. *They* entered me in the race."

"But why?" Melvin asked, rolling his eyes.

I curled my lip. "Because they want revenge."

"You mean that the Scavengers are seeking vengeance by having you run for class president? That sounds a little… over the top."

I nodded slowly, staring at the reporter with the most intense eyes I could muster.

"Do you know how *coconuts* that sounds?" Melvin asked,

not even trying to hide a smile. He started speaking with a lower voice while bobbing his head back and forth, impersonating what he thought a Scavenger sounded like. "*Oh, we hate Chase Cooper. Here's an idea! Let's have him run for president! That'll teach him a lesson! Oh, the sweet taste of revenge!*"

"Whatever, dude."

"Man, if *that's* how the Scavengers get their revenge," Melvin said. "Then sign me up! How can *I* make them angry too?"

I folded my arms and pushed against the back of my chair... yes, like a baby. "It's because I exposed Sebastian for lying to the students and staff last week."

Melvin lifted his head steadily. "Because why? Sebastian was a Scavenger?"

"Yup."

The reporter pushed his lips to the side of his face and lifted an eyebrow. With a thumbs-up, he sarcastically said, "Yeah, *okay.* That sounds like something that would happen."

"Again," I said. "You think it sounds crazy, but you're looking for *ninjas* in the school! Tell me *that's* not crazy!"

"Ninjas are a totally different animal," Melvin said. "Plus there's already photographic evidence that they exist."

"Just a kid in a Halloween costume," I said. Hopefully the reporter couldn't see through my lies.

"Maybe, but that doesn't make them any less of a ninja. So tell me, Chase Cooper. Why would *I* receive a text message telling me to follow *you* if I wanted to learn the truth about the Buchanan ninjas?"

"What's your beef with ninjas anyway?" I asked.

Melvin paused, and then he spoke under his breath. "My father was... *kidnapped* by ninjas."

I stared in disbelief. "Whaaaaaaaat?"

"No, I'm joking," Melvin laughed. "But seriously, ninjas are dangerous, and the fact that they're hiding in our school is bad. Ninjas *aren't* good guys."

"What if *these* ninjas are?"

"So you're saying there *are* ninjas in the school?"

I cleared my throat. "No. I'm just saying that maybe you should consider it a possibility that you're wrong. Maybe not all ninjas are bad. Maybe the Scavengers are real. As a reporter, shouldn't you consider every angle?"

Melvin scribbled in his notepad. "Fair enough."

The door to the room swung open. Mr. Lien stepped in and snatched some papers from his desk. He looked up, surprised to see Melvin. "Excuse me? What're you doing in here?"

"Buchanan Press," Melvin said boldly.

"I don't care if you're the president of the school," the teacher snipped. "If you're not supposed to be in here, get out!"

Flipping his notepad shut, Melvin jumped from his seat. Before leaving the room, he turned one last time. "We'll continue this later."

Fantastic. Just *another* thing to look forward to.

That was sarcastic… in case you couldn't tell.

Thursday. 7:35 AM. Before school.

The next morning, I crammed my book bag into my locker. Since I was going to be on the cleanup crew all day, I figured I didn't need anything with me.

I passed Brayden in the hallway, but he didn't even acknowledge my existence. His eyes looked right through me like I was the Invisible Woman. Wait… why didn't I say the Invisible Man?

Anyway, a dirty look I can handle. Saying something mean I can handle. Even getting punched in the face I can *kind* of handle. But acting like I didn't even exist was far worse than any of those other things.

When I stepped into the lobby, a bunch of kids cheered my name for president. "*Coopster for president!*" they said, but I just wasn't into it. All I wanted was for Friday night to come along so I could loose myself in videogames and comic books. The weekend was starting to sound really good, but that was still two days away.

Suddenly, a kid from Jake's wolf pack shoulder bumped me, but it wasn't on purpose. He was cutting across the lobby with his eyes set on the student he was hunting. It was one of the meaner members of Jake's posse. His name was Devon, and he looked like he was on a mission.

Across the room, I saw Melvin drinking from a water fountain – the one where the water barely makes it above the spigot so you practically have to make out with the water fountain if you want a drink. So gross.

84

I let out a heavy sigh. As much as Melvin was getting on my nerves, I still didn't want the kid to get hurt, especially since he was clueless about the danger he was flirting with.

Keeping my head down, I followed Devon as he weaved between students in the busy lobby.

Melvin slurped at the water like a thirsty dog. His ginormous camera slung over his shoulder, resting at his side.

As Devon got closer, I sped my pace, cutting around a few students so I could pass him without being seen. In his hand was a roll of duct tape, probably for taping Melvin to a wall. What a weird thing for bullies to do.

At about ten feet away, Melvin finally rose from the water fountain. Using his shirtsleeve, he wiped the water from his mouth and began turning around.

I heard the ripping sound of duct tape as Devon raised his hands higher. There wasn't any time left. I had to act fast.

Jumping through an open spot in the crowd, I landed in front of the bully, blocking his path to Melvin. I grabbed the strap of tape in Devon's hands before he knew what was happening.

Spinning a circle in the hall, I rolled my fists around both of Devon's wrists. Since I was spinning, I rolled the tape around his hands once when they were in front of me, and then again when they were behind me, and finally one last time when they were in front of me again. It was almost like I was dancing.

I had used Devon's own trap against him.

"Hey!" Devon grunted.

We were still moving forward so all I had to do was nudge him one time when we were passed the water fountain. He lumbered into the women's bathroom door, pushing it open, and falling inside.

The screams and shouts from the girl's bathroom made me laugh, but also made sure Devon was gonna get busted.

A small crowd gathered around the bathroom door as I walked away from it. Melvin was clear down the hallway, completely clueless that I had saved him from trouble a second time.

Thursday. 7:45 AM. Detention.

Principal Davis had assigned me cleanup duty for the day, which meant exactly what it sounded like. I was going to be parading around the school grounds wearing an orange vest and hat, picking up random bits of litter here and there. Super fun, right?

I was slipping the vest over my shoulders when Mr. Lien stepped into the room. He was carrying a box with empty trash bags and one of those long handles with a set of pinchers on the end that people used to pick up garbage without bending over. I gotta be honest – I was excited to play with the pincher stick.

In the hall, I heard someone dash by the front door, dropping a large stack of papers in front of the room. It was probably the school paper. Melvin didn't have the goods on the ninjas yet so I wasn't worried about any articles he might've written.

Mr. Lien pointed at the desk I had sat at the day before. "You've got a package over there. I believe it's all your assignments you'll miss since you're out of classes for the day."

I studied the package, which was about the size of a shoebox. No way a day's worth of homework could fill such a huge container.

"As soon as you're ready, you're free to walk the schoolyard and pick up trash," Mr. Lien said before he stepped out.

"Gotcha," I replied, waiting for the teacher to return to his class across the hall. Finally, I was alone with the mystery box.

86

Stepping up to the package, I jabbed at it with my finger. Whatever was inside wasn't heavy because the box spun in a half circle.

Pulling on the lid of the box, I ripped it away from the rectangular tape that was holding it in place. I stared, confused about what I was seeing.

Sitting on top of several folded sheets of paper was a note I had written to Faith a few months back. Some might call it a "love" note, but I like to call it a "like" note. Get it? You don't fall "in love" until you're an adult. You only fall "in like" before that. Whatever, I'm a dork.

I took my note out of the box, surprised to see it. When I brought it closer to my face, I saw that it wasn't my actual note I had written, but instead, it was a photocopy.

Tipping the box over, I emptied the rest of the folded sheets of paper onto the desk. They were all black and white photocopies of love notes from random students in the school. I was standing above a gossip treasure chest.

The television in the hallway flipped on, playing music

through the school's speaker system. As I approached the open door to the detention room, I listened to the message that the whole school was hearing.

"Buchanan School…" the narrator started. It was the same voice that was in the video about Brayden. "A place where friendships are tested in the waters of gossip and rumors. A place where secrets can tear apart relationships the same way babies do with a bag of chips."

My face – my goofy and smiling face – slowly appeared on the screen. I wasn't surprised.

What were the Scavengers going to say today? What friend were they going to try to take away from me this time?

The narrator continued. "Which is why Chase Cooper has promised to *end* all secrets. If nobody has secrets, then we're one big happy family. That's what Chase is offering to the school!"

"Zoinks" I whispered. "Did I just say '*zoinks?*' Who am I even talking to?"

"That's why the Chase Cooper newsletter has been distributed to everyone everywhere!" The voice said enthusiastically. "It highlights the juiciest secrets that your friends have to offer! Read up, kids! A friend who keeps secrets, isn't a friend at all! So let's *all* be BFFs! You're welcome, Buchanan. You're welcome."

I looked down at the stack of papers that were dropped off by the front door before class started. It wasn't the school paper I was staring at. It was "The Chase Cooper Newsletter of Secrets," complete with a huge bold title and everything.

The video started to fade out, but not before my recorded voice played over the speakers again. "*My name is Chase Cooper, and I approve this message.*"

Holy. Stromboli.

I knew it was bad because just on the front page, I could see several secrets highlighted. The ones that stuck out were the ones about the people I knew.

Naomi has kissed a boy.
Brayden sleeps with a nightlight.
Jake has an unnatural fear of clowns.
Gavin barfs at the sight of barf.

Olivia Jones pretends to be a villain named Jovial Noise.
Wyatt wet the bed until he was seven-years-old.

The list went on when I unfolded the newspaper. This was *bad. Super* bad. Bad like, *end-of-the-world-because-the-sun-just-exploded* bad.

I could hear shrieks of terror echo down the hall as students poured from their classrooms. Homeroom wasn't over, but that didn't stop them from leaving their rooms.

Slinking back into detention, I shut the door quietly, locking it from the inside. I could hear the mob grow angrier through the thin walls of the room.

So that's the friend the Scavengers were going to take from me – *all of them.*

Thursday. 11:30 AM. Lunch.

I waited until first period started before I left the detention room. Mr. Lien didn't even try to convince me to come out earlier. In fact, he *encouraged* me to stay in there all day, but being in a tiny room like that made me feel like a caged animal. If there was anything I needed, it was some fresh air. I made a deal with Mr. Lien to stay out of sight at least until lunch.

Principal Davis made sure all the Chase Cooper Newsletters were rounded up and stored them away in the detention room until they could be properly recycled.

But I had to get away from the smell of the newsprint. They were musty, and reeked of burnt ink. Whatever the ink was that they used was weird. I'm sure the ink would be settled on the newsprint within a couple of hours, but it was still fresh enough that it got all over my fingers, which then got *everywhere.* My book bag, clothing, and face had black streak marks all over them. I looked like I cleaned chimneys for a living.

The only good thing about being painted up like a soldier was that nobody recognized me when I walked to the kitchen.

But even though they didn't see me, they still talked about me.

"Can't believe Chase would do such an awful thing."

"Right? He better get expelled or I'm going to petition."

"If we get enough signatures, I bet we could make it happen!"

Geez. Crazy how fast fans can turn to haters.

Grabbing my yellow lunch tray, I stepped out of the kitchen and into the cafeteria. I stood in the doorway for a second, waiting to see if anyone would know it was me. I was safe since my face had newspaper ink all over it. Not much of a disguise, but it seemed to be working.

At the far corner of the cafeteria, I found an empty table and sat, but didn't feel hungry. It was fried chicken leg day anyway – not my favorite food.

"Eating in the cafeteria?" Naomi asked, appearing out of nowhere. She stood over me with her hands behind her back. "Awfully brave of you."

I winced. Apparently the printer ink on my face *wasn't* enough of a disguise. "Is it obvious that it's me?"

Naomi smiled. "Nah," she said softly. "Just to me. I could tell it was you if you were wearing a gorilla costume." Studying me with her eyes, her expression softened like she felt sorry for me. "But man, you look *terrible*. How'd your clothes get all dirty?"

"Detention will do that to ya," I said. "I've *seen* things, Naomi. *Sickening* things."

"Like what?"

"A dead mouse."

"Ew, *barf-aroni!* Really?"

"Well, not the actual dead mouse itself," I said. "But I could smell it. Have you ever smelled a dead mouse? That's not somethin' you can easily come back from."

"Well, ya look like you painted your face to play some football," Naomi said.

"Yeah, because that sounds like me," I said, looking at my fingers. "No, I got newspaper ink all over my hands from that dumb Chase Cooper Newsletter that was passed around this morning. The ink was all powdery and messy still. It's impossible to get off and gets *everywhere*."

"Oh?" Naomi said, lifting an eyebrow. "I wouldn't know. I didn't touch any of those papers."

I let out a sigh. "Man, I wish I didn't touch any either."

"So it wasn't you that printed them?" Naomi asked jokingly.

"*Really?*" I replied.

Out of nowhere, a mound of wet mashed potatoes exploded on the table next to us. Other students at nearby tables turned in their seats to see what had made the *splut* sound.

Someone shouted from across the room. "Hey, everybody! It's the Coopster! The Coopster's dumb enough to eat lunch in here!"

Chicken legs started traveling in my direction – probably the only food *designed* to be chucked across a vast open space. They were like fried grenades sailing across a battlefield of frustrated ADHD-diagnosed sixth graders. I was just thankful that nobody had good aim.

"Get out of here, loser!" a girl shouted. "Because of you, everyone knows I had head lice in third grade! My boyfriend dumped me after he read that in your little gossip magazine!"

Everyone started screaming at the same time. I could only make out small bits of sentences here and there, but everyone was shouting about how much they hated me.

92

Pushing my tray aside, I jumped from the table.

I heard Naomi yell for me, but I didn't slow down. I ran all the way down the side of the cafeteria, dodging handfuls of food and ignoring the angry howls from the mob that had formed in the lunchroom.

Slamming my body into the door, I stumbled into the lobby, safe from the other students. But that wasn't far enough for me. Keeping my face down, I escaped into one of the bathrooms nearby.

My heart was pumping so hard that my eyes could *see* it. Every pump of blood made the lights in the bathroom dim just a little. I could count my pulse by watching the shadows on the wall.

Sliding my hand against the wall helped me from falling over, but my knees were starting to feel weak. I kicked open one of the stall doors and locked it shut.

My mouth started watering like crazy, and then I finally did what I had always been afraid of doing in school.

I barfed.

Good thing I was already in the stall, right?

It wasn't much, but it didn't have to be for me to feel *wrecked*. Flushing the toilet, I climbed up and sat on the tank, wiping my mouth with toilet paper and catching my breath.

It was at that moment when I heard the door to the men's room swing open.

I swallowed hard, and waited patiently for whoever it was to do their business and leave. If I just sat silently, they wouldn't even know I was in there.

Except that whoever it was knocked on the stall door that I was in.

I froze. Even on a normal day, if someone knocked on a bathroom stall door that I was in, I would freak out. I mumbled. "Uh, um… occupied," I said, staring at the kid's bright red tennis shoes that were standing at the foot of the stall door.

And then the most bizarre thing happened. The latch to the stall I was in slowly started moving to the left on its own. The door was unlocking itself.

Clunk.

All I could do was stare at the door as it slowly opened.

On the other side stood a boy, at least I think it was a boy, wearing one of the Scavenger's vulture masks. He was holding a rectangular magnet. That must be how he managed to slide the lock open from the outside of the door.

"Dude," I said, getting more upset that someone had just opened my *locked* stall door. "*What if I was in here droppin' the kids off at the pool?*"

The vulture mask tilted, the same way a dog's head does when they're confused. "Kids? Pool?"

"Number two!" I snapped.

"Oh," the boy said, shaking his head. "I dunno. I'm only here to deliver a message."

"They told you to deliver it while I was on the John?" I growled. "That's insane."

"It is what it is," the boy replied.

"But what if it isn't what it is?" I asked. "Or wasn't what it used to be, but became what it was supposed to be?"

The Scavenger held his open palm out to me, motioning for

me to stop. "Please," he said, shaking his head. "You're going to make my brain cry."

"Who's your leader?" I asked, hoping the boy would be confused enough to answer without thinking.

The boy in the mask ignored my question, stuttering just a bit as he spoke. It sounded as if he were reciting something he memorized. "If... if you *tell* on us, then we'll move in on your friends. Zoe, Faith, Brayden, Naomi, and Gavin."

I could feel my blood boiling under my skin when he listed my friends by name.

"The rest of them will all fall victim to the wrath of the Scavengers," the masked boy said. "We'll allow you to lose with *some* shred of your dignity left. We'll end this game with you, leaving your friends alone, *if* you accept defeat."

I leaned back against the cold wall, staring at the eyes of the boy in the mask.

He continued to stutter as he tried to remember his scripted message. "Become the 'nobody' that you should've been when you showed up on the first day of school. You should've kept to yourself at that time."

My eyes drifted to the floor as I listened.

"We're giving you a second chance to become *nothing*," the boy said. "To be the student that should've just disappeared in a sea of other students."

I clenched my jaw as the masked kid shut the stall door. His feet stomped across the bathroom until the door to the restroom creaked open. I heard the noise from students in the hall, waiting for lunch to end. Then it was silent again.

My throat dried as I stared at nothing. The quiet and stillness of the empty restroom felt like it was going to crush my head so I flushed the toilet again, just to hear *something*.

The Scavengers had done what no other student had done to me – destroyed my reputation. But they did it in a way that I couldn't even fight back. I felt completely helpless and lost sitting alone in the bathroom stall.

But I didn't want it to end like that.

Squeezing my eyes shut as tight as I could, I felt a surge of energy travel down my back. *Why* couldn't I fight back? *Why* couldn't I do something about all that?

Of course if I hid away in the bathroom then *nothing* would change! I was in charge of my own destiny, and I wasn't about to let a bunch of kids wearing ugly bird masks get the best of me!

I booted the stall door open and ran to the entrance of the bathroom. If I hurried, I could probably see the boy who delivered the message still walking away. At that point, he would've removed the vulture mask, but I'd still be able to recognize his bright red shoes.

When I pushed open the bathroom door, I felt like I was ready to take on the world, but it wasn't the world that was waiting on the other side in the lobby. It was Jake and Wyatt.

Instantly, Jake shoved me back onto the wall. "I hope you didn't think I forgot about all the payback I owed you, didja? I was just waiting for the right time!"

Wyatt stood like a statue behind Jake. "You're gonna pay so bad for that paper you put out this morning! The fact that I wet my bed until I was seven is nobody's business but my own!"

"Tell him, babe!" muttered Olive. As a crowd of students started gathering around us, I couldn't see her anymore, but I heard her start chanting again. "Wy-att! Wy-att! Wy-att!"

I tried to respond, but it only came out as a jumble of vowels. My thoughts were drowning out any quirky comeback I tried to think of.

Instead of letting myself get pummeled, I rolled to my feet, dashing for the cafeteria door. I wasn't sure how many times I'd been involved in a chase within the walls of Buchanan School, but I knew it was going to be at least once more.

As I reached for the handle of the cafeteria door, I made an escape plan in my head. I was going to pull a sharp right turn after jumping through the entrance. After that, I'd sprint toward the stage. A sharp left turn would put me on a clear path to the exit at the back of the cafeteria. All I had to do was make it to the exit so I could get outside. Then it would be smooth sailing from there…

But it's funny how a small bump can toss an entire escape plan into the dumpster.

Just before I touched the handle to the cafeteria door, I felt someone push me. Since I was already running at full speed, I couldn't stop myself. My face banged against the wooden door as my body crashed through the entrance.

I managed to keep myself on my feet, but not without looking like a puppet that was being forced to dance for a roomful of students.

Finally, because the universe hates me, I slammed into one of the lunch tables, which sent me flying over the top of it like a stuntman earning his salary.

On my back, I stared at the ceiling of the school, listening to the roar of laughter erupting from my sixth grade peers.

The faces of kids became blurs as I blinked, trying to keep a straight face through the sharp pain of getting tossed around like a ragdoll.

The worst part about it? I knew it was all *my* fault – all of it. If I had just minded my own business at the beginning of the year, I wouldn't be the laughing stock of the whole lunchroom. I wouldn't be on my back contemplating a transfer to another school. I wouldn't be running my tongue over all my teeth, making sure none of them were missing.

Basically, I wouldn't have any troubles.

As I forced myself off the ground, I could hear every insult that everyone was throwing at me. I'm sure there were teachers that were trying to help me, but the crowd of spectators was so thick that it didn't make it easy.

Zoe pushed through the mob, and stopped just at the edge of it. "Chase...?"

I couldn't stand it anymore. The embarrassment was just too heavy and maddening that I ran to the stage at the front of the room. I rolled across the wood and escaped under the red velvet curtain.

But I could still hear everyone's laughter and taunts so I continued until I was as far backstage as I could go.

There in the dark, I leaned against one of the wooden storage boxes. It sucks saying this, but I was trying my hardest to hold in my tears. With my luck, if I started crying, the curtains would split open and a spotlight would shine on me.

Suddenly footsteps pounded on the stage, but they weren't close. I pushed my back against the box, making myself as small as possible so I wouldn't be seen.

Whoever was running was panting heavily. I peeked over the box to see what was going on.

Across the stage, Melvin was running at full speed, his camera swinging wildly on his shoulder. Behind him were two red ninjas.

I slapped the wooden floor of the stage, frustrated. My brain started arguing with me as I tried to shut out the sound of Melvin's footsteps.

Go help him!

"Why?" I asked aloud.

Y'know, ninja honor and stuff.

"I mean, I *know* why! But *why* should I bother? Everyone at this school *hates* me!"

So what? This isn't about who hates you and who doesn't! This is about doing the right thing, even when you don't feel like it!

"But what's the right thing?" I asked, like I was actually talking to someone. "What if sitting here was the right thing? What if doing *nothing* to help him is the right thing? Hmm?"

If you don't help Melvin, I'm going to make you think of your parents kissing!

"Gross, dude!"

I swear I'll do it!

"Whatever, dumb-hole! You can't make me do that!"

Oh really? Watch this – DON'T think of your parents kissing!

My pupils dilated as the world went black. "*Noooooooooooo!*"

Now go!

I paused, pulling my ninja mask over my face. "What if he doesn't even need help?"

My brain didn't answer.

I furrowed my brow, looking up like I was going to actually see my own brain. I shook my head, realizing how insane I must've looked.

I grunted, picking myself up off the floor. Melvin might've been an annoying insect, but he didn't deserve to get beat up for doing his job – nobody did... unless their job was pro-wrestling, but last I checked, Melvin *wasn't* a pro-wrestler.

Unless he was a *secret* pro-wrestler that was parading around as a – nope, nevermind.

I glanced down the short corridor that the red ninjas had chased Melvin down. It was a hallway full of exits, but I could hear their footsteps still. It meant Wyatt and Jake were back there, and probably gaining on the reporter.

I took off running toward the sound of the steps. "It's go-time."

Thursday. 12:00 PM. Way backstage.

"Melvin, Melvin, Melvin," sighed one of the red ninjas. "We've warned you *many* times this week! You've *had* the chance to just... *forget* about it, but you chose not to."

"The students of the school need to know the truth!" Melvin shouted, hanging upside-down. "I *knew* there were ninjas in the school! I totally called it!"

The two red ninjas had already caught the reporter. Melvin had a thick rope tied around his ankle that was slung over one of the overhead catwalks. The place where the red ninjas had tied the knot was only a couple feet away from me.

I was sticking to the shadows on the catwalk, looking down on the red ninjas and the reporter. I didn't have a plan, but I knew I needed one quick or else Melvin was going to pass out from hanging upside-down.

One of the red ninjas pushed on the reporter's body, making him swing back and forth slowly. "Ever heard of a piñata?" the red ninja snarled. "I wonder... will you spill some candy if we pop you open?"

The other ninja chuckled, keeping his arms folded. It looked as bizarre and evil as it sounded.

"You know," the first ninja said, kneeling closer to Melvin's face. "Our ninja clan could use a new punching bag."

"You think can get away with this?" Melvin asked, his voice shaking.

The two ninjas all looked at each other. After a few nods

back and forth, the shorter ninja looked at Melvin. "Yeah," he said. "Yeah, we do."

I knew who the ninjas were from their voices, especially since I had just dealt with them in the lobby. It was Wyatt, the leader of the red ninjas, and Jake, the leader of the wolf pack.

Quickly and quietly, I untied the knot on the thick rope next to me. I had to wrap it around my arm a few times. With my feet, I propped myself against the catwalk so I could carry Melvin's weight without him dropping to the floor.

Melvin's super fat camera was on the ground, just out of his reach. The shorter ninja, Wyatt, danced over to it. "Don't think you'll be needing *this* anymore!" he sang as he booted it like he was trying to score a soccer goal.

The old camera shot across the floor until smashing to pieces against a brick wall. A flash of light and a puff of smoke burst from the camera.

"No!" Melvin shouted. "That thing was an antique!"

103

"Get with the times!" Jake hissed. "Use a camera phone like everyone else in the world!"

"I *have* a camera phone," Melvin said. "But I prefer the old school one over it!"

Wyatt chuckled. "The eighteen-hundreds called, Mel! They want their camera back!"

Melvin's face was growing red, maybe from being angry, but probably from hanging upside-down too long. "Gross, my dad called – he wants his lame joke back."

I couldn't see Wyatt's face, but I knew Melvin's comment had instantly angered him from the way his posture changed. He planted one foot behind him. "Insulting me is the last mistake you'll ever make!"

That was it – the sign that things had escalated from a mean prank to DEFCON 1.

Holding tight to the rope with both of my hands, I did one of the most dangerously irresponsible things in my life. I jumped over the side of the catwalk.

I instantly regretted it, crying out in fear.

"Gaaaaaaaaaaaaah! Look out!"

If this were a movie, I would've landed on my feet, using Melvin's weight to counter my own to allow for a smooth descent. But since this was real life, I just dropped like a potato.

Melvin's weight on the other end of the rope was at least enough that I didn't break any bones. That, plus landing on top of him probably helped too. It was clumsy, awkward, and painful.

But it was awesome.

Wyatt and Jake stepped back, surprised by my sudden ninja-like entrance.

Melvin whimpered under me. It's possible that I might've done more damage to him than Jake and Wyatt were going to do.

"Sorry, man," I said. "Please don't be dead."

The reporter pushed me off of him. "Get off me!"

Rolling to my feet, I stuck out my chest and stared at the two red ninjas.

The confusion left Wyatt's eyes – it was almost like I could see the light bulb switch on in his head. "Enjoy your trip back in the cafeteria?"

I couldn't think of a good comeback, so instead, I said, "Not really."

Jake stepped forward, his muffled voice speaking through his red ninja mask. "Why are you protecting Melvin? Don't you understand that this involves *both* our ninja clans? If he exposes one, then he exposes *both*! Don't you want to stop him?"

"I'm not a fan of Melvin's intentions," I said. "But *this* isn't the way to stop him."

Wyatt chuckled. "You think asking nicely will work?" He leaned over, resting his hands on his knees and spoke to Melvin as if he were a baby. "Pwetty pwease, with sugah on top?"

Melvin's stare grew intense, but he didn't say anything.

Suddenly, Jake pushed me hard. I stumbled, trying to avoid Melvin, but couldn't. Tripping over his body, I fell against the wooden floor.

Instantly, Melvin jumped up, grabbing my arm and helping me to my feet. "Hit them back! Give them what they deserve!"

I didn't care to tell Melvin my belief that punches should

never be thrown, so instead, I said nothing while walking backwards keeping the reporter behind me.

Wyatt jumped through the air, coming at me with his legs scissor kicking like a weird looking flamingo. He even made the same sound a flamingo would make, but I'm not a hundred percent sure about that – I'm not an expert on flamingos.

Turning, I pushed Melvin back, trying to keep him safe from the attack. The reporter grabbed my hoodie, clinging to me like a child. Because of that, I hobbled over him, tripping again.

That time I managed to keep myself up by taking large steps, but just as I had caught my balance, Jake slammed into both the reporter and me.

We fumbled into the door at the side of the room. It was old and crusty so instead of breaking *our* fall, we broke the door.

Wood splintered everywhere as Melvin and I crashed into the next room.

Someone screamed, frightened by our sudden appearance.

I'm not surprised – kids crashing through walls wasn't something you'd see everyday.

"Where are we?" I asked, rubbing my head.

"The voting room," Melvin said as he lay on his back.

At the far corner of the room, Daisy was holding a cardboard box upside-down, dumping a ton of pink slips into a giant red machine.

"Daisy?" I asked through my ninja mask.

Before she could answer, Jake and Wyatt stepped into the room still decked out in their red ninja gear.

Daisy's eyes peeled open like a cartoon, and she let out the worst scream I'd ever heard in my life.

Melvin scooted his butt across the floor as he tried to get away from the two red ninja nutcases that were after him. At that point, he had taken his cell phone out of his pocket and was snapping pictures with it. Bright flashes flooded my vision as I tried to make sense of what was happening.

"Leave him alone!" I shouted, rising off the floor.

The taller of the two ninjas, Jake, turned and threw a roundhouse kick in my direction. If I were closer, it probably would've done some damage, but since I was just out of reach, his foot swung wildly, unable to stop. It was like when a kid swings a baseball bat too hard, but misses the ball. Jake made himself lose balance and spilled to the floor.

"*Nothin' but net!*" I said like an announcer.

All of the commotion in the room halted. Everyone looked at me like they were confused.

Even Daisy, who was crouched down and picking up her pink slips, stopped to look at me.

"I think 'nothin' but net' would mean that the ninja totally kicked you," Melvin said.

Wyatt nodded. "'Nothin' but net' is normally a good thing."

"Oh," I said, scratching the back of my head. "Um, so..."

"I think you meant to say 'air ball,'" Melvin said.

I snapped my fingers at the reporter. "That's it! That's what I meant! *Aiiiiir ball!*"

Jake picked himself up off the ground. "Can we continue this then?"

I looked at Melvin and shrugged my shoulders. Melvin

looked at Wyatt as they both nodded.

It was such a strange pause in all the action that I honestly believe the whole fight would've ended there if it weren't for the girl who sparked the flame back into a fire.

Daisy tossed her cardboard box on the ground and ran for the exit. Several slips of pink paper fell from her box. Wyatt ignored the reporter and instead moved toward Daisy.

"No!" Daisy screamed, reaching for the handle.

I was too far to do anything.

Suddenly, the exit door flipped open. Someone on the outside must've opened it because it swung out before Daisy even touched it. As soon as she jumped out, the door slammed shut again.

Wyatt slid to a stop, confused. He stared at the door like it was going to open again, but it didn't, not yet.

Melvin continued to cower in the corner snapping photos from his phone, which was fine by me as long as he stayed out of the way.

Jake was beginning to panic too.

I was on the floor, frozen in place because I was confused as heck, which is why I didn't notice when Jake started moving toward Melvin until the very last second.

"Help!" Melvin shouted as he continued snapping pictures of Jake.

I dashed across the room. I wasn't sure what my plan was, but I didn't have time to think about it.

With my arms in front of me, I jumped at Jake, but he was ready for me. After I landed on the ground, he ignored me, continuing his pursuit of Melvin.

"Gimme that phone!" Jake shouted as he raised his fists.

I grabbed Jake's ankle and yanked him off his balance. He whipped his hands out behind him to keep himself from falling. He glared at me through his mask. "I am *so* sick of you being *everywhere*!"

He reached his hand toward Melvin's camera, but I jumped in the way. Instead of grabbing the reporter's phone, he grabbed the top of my mask and clenched his fist. The fabric pulled up on my nose and eyelids.

"You want a story?" Jake sneered at Melvin. "How's *this* for a story."

Then the red ninja ripped my ninja mask off my face. The blast of cold air from the room spread over my cheeks as I heard Melvin gasp.

I pushed Jake off me, but he didn't care. He was laughing as he stumbled backward, gripping my black ninja mask in his hand.

Melvin's jaw was dropped. He was shocked, but not shocked enough to stop taking pics. With his camera phone aimed at my face, he continued to snap photos for his article.

Wyatt clenched his fists, glaring at Jake. The really weird thing about Wyatt was that while he was an evil dude, there were still rules he followed. I found out a couple weeks ago that one of those rules was that he would never reveal the identity of another ninja, even if that ninja was me.

It's the ninja-code, which is like the bro-code, but with ninjas… except the bro-code means you don't date your best friend's ex-girlfriend sooooooo… the ninja-code is nothing like that.

Jake had just crossed the line with Wyatt.

A cloud of white chalk dust exploded at the entrance. I heard the entrance door swing open, along with the sound of several people shuffling around. At last, the door clicked again, closing.

As the dust lifted, black silhouettes came into view. There must have been at least ten shadows standing near the entrance with their arms folded.

After another second, it was clear that the room was filled with new ninjas – *my* ninjas. That must've been why Wyatt was shocked earlier – he must've caught a glimpse of them when they opened the door for Daisy.

"Leave," said one of the members of my ninja clan. "You don't want none of this."

Jake lifted the bottom part of his mask and spit on the ground. He dropped my ninja mask. "Next time use less chalk. It's bad for the lungs."

Wyatt wasn't about to try his odds against ten members of my ninja clan. He held his fingers up to Jake, signaling him to keep his mouth shut. Without saying another word, Wyatt stepped back through the door we had shattered, into the next room where they had been picking on Melvin.

Jake followed, but not before shooting Melvin one last look.

Once they were gone, I approached the members of my ninja clan. "How'd you guys know we were in here?"

One of the ninjas hesitated. "Master..."

I could tell he was hiding something. "What is it?" I asked.

"This will be the last time we help you," the ninja said, not sadly, but softly, like it was something he didn't want to say but needed to.

I looked at him, confused.

At that second, Melvin finally got the moment he had been waiting for. He grabbed several of the pink slips Daisy had dropped, and darted for the exit. Jumping through my ninja clan, he disappeared into the hall.

Thursday. 12:15 PM. The hallway

"Wait!" I shouted, reaching my hand out like I was going to use the Force to stop Melvin. I squeezed my hand shut, embarrassed. "Dangit!"

I pushed through my ninja clan and ran into the lobby. "Stay outta sight!" I said to my ninjas as I chased after Melvin. "Melvin, stop! Wait!"

Melvin might've responded, but if he did, I couldn't tell what he said since it was masked by his high-pitched wheezing.

"Let me explain this to you!" I shouted as I sprinted after the reporter. At the end of the hallway, I cut the corner without slowing down so I could keep up. "Melvin, stop! I just want to talk to –"

And then *KA-BAM!*

My skull met another kid's skull, but not in the "It's nice to meet you!" sort of way. It was more of the "OMG, did you see that?? Let me rewind the video so you can see it again! Watch, watch, watch, annnnnnd... *Ohhhhhhhhhhhhh!*" kind of way.

The flash of pain was blinding as I spilled to the floor. I heard a girl cry out in pain as she bumped against the metal lockers behind her. When the stars cleared from my vision, I saw Naomi leaning against the wall, holding her head.

"Thanks for that," Naomi said, keeping her eyes shut. "I don't really understand why you still insist on running around corners at warp speed? You'd think that you would've learned to stop after the first time you crashed into someone."

"I was running after Melvin," I said, pinching the bottom of nose, hoping that blood wouldn't start pouring out of it. "Did you see him run back here?"

Naomi rubbed her forehead. "Maybe? I'm having a hard time remembering anything before you body-checked me."

I laughed, but realized she might not have been joking. "Serious?"

"No," Naomi said. "I'm not serious."

I crawled across the cold floor toward my friend's book bag that was crumpled on the linoleum next to us. "Sorry about that," I said.

Massaging the spot between her eyes, Naomi spoke. "It's fine," she said. "Too bad Melvin got away."

I started scooping up Naomi's notebooks and gel pens. "Yeah," I said. "And he totally saw my face. I have to find him. If I don't, he might publish something that'll ruin my life… not like it's not already—" I stopped speaking when I pulled Naomi's book bag open to put her stuff away.

My face grew hot as I stared slack-jawed into my friend's bag. Resting at the bottom of the canvas sack was a vulture mask. It was the same kind that the Scavengers wore.

Naomi opened her eyes. "What's—" she stopped when she saw my face. Then she calmly spoke. "Are you gaping at the vulture mask? It's one of the masks you got in that package at the beginning of the week."

I felt a wave of relief wash over me, but the feeling quickly faded when I remembered that I had snapped both of those masks in half. "But I broke those…" I said softly. "And then I tossed them into the trash."

Naomi flipped over and crawled closer to me. Grabbed my wrist with her hand, she pulled my arm away from her bag. "I know," she said without missing a beat. "I got one out of the garbage can after you threw them away. I took it home and fixed it."

"But why?" I asked, puzzled.

"In case you needed it again," Naomi said, softly smiling, gazing into my eyes like a lost kitten. Naomi had a tear forming in her eye. It was almost like she *wanted* me to see she was crying.

"I'm sorry about running into you," I said.

Naomi nodded, wiping the tear from her face.

A black streak appeared on her cheek where her thumb had rubbed. "You got some…" I started saying, lifting my thumb to Naomi's face. I tried to clean the black spot off, but I only made it worse. I still had all the ink from the Chase Cooper Newsletters that had been spread across the school that morning. Funny enough, the black streak I left on Naomi's cheek matched the streak she had left with her own thumb. In fact, they even spread over her skin exactly the same way…

Wait… what?

I stared into Naomi's eyes with my hand still on her cheek. Then I glanced at the spot on my wrist where she had pulled me away from her bag – a black powdery ink was smeared there too.

"Dude," she said, leaning away from me. "You can let go of my cheek now, ya creeper."

My words dried up in my throat as I stared at Naomi's hands. She had a black residue on her fingertips and under her nails. My heart started racing.

"Back in the cafeteria," I said. "You told me you didn't touch any of the gossip newspapers."

Naomi paused. "I didn't touch 'em."

114

"The funny thing about newspaper ink," I said, "is that it's impossible to get off... and it gets *everywhere*."

Naomi looked at her hands, and then changed the story. "Oh, I mean, I might've picked up a copy after I talked to you in the cafeteria."

"All the copies have been hidden away though. Principal Davis made sure of that."

"Not all of them," Naomi said defensively.

My brain was stuck. I didn't know what else to say. "Naomi... you're just making yourself sound *more* guilty."

My friend's expression completely shifted. Her posture straightened as her eyes stared daggers back at me. She zipped up her book bag and stood from the ground, slinging the bag over her right shoulder.

I waited for Naomi to explain herself, but she didn't.

Instead, she turned around and started walking down the hall.

"Naomi!" I said, standing up.

She didn't answer.

"Naomi, stop!" I said, following her. "Please! Why's that mask in your bag?"

Again, she didn't answer. She didn't even look over her shoulder at me. It was like I wasn't even there.

I jogged to catch up. Staying a few feet behind my friend, I pleaded with her because I didn't *want* my suspicion to be correct. I couldn't stand the thought that was repeating in my noggin.

I didn't want my friend to be a Scavenger!

I grabbed her arm. "Please talk to me!"

Naomi spun halfway around, raising her elbow so that it was above my hand. Then she dropped her elbow straight down, pulling free from my grip. After spinning halfway around again, she continued her robotic walk down the hall.

Standing still in the middle of the corridor, I watched as my friend, maybe one of my *best* friends, ignored me.

At the end of the hall, she turned to her right and opened one of the doors. She glanced once at me before stepping through. But instead of shutting the door behind her, she left it wide open like she *wanted* me to follow her.

I could barely feel my legs as I hurried to the open door. I wasn't sure what to expect in the dark room. All I knew was that Naomi was in there.

I didn't have to think about it, and stepped into the unknown.

Thursday. 12:30 PM. An unknown classroom.

"Naomi?" I whispered, walking farther into the dark classroom. It was one of the rooms that was at the center of the school so there weren't any windows to the outside to allow the sun to shine in. The light switch on the wall didn't work either. I flipped it a couple times to make sure.

From the light in the hallway I could see some props leaning against the walls. It looked like maybe I was in one of the rooms that had theater class. There were cardboard cutouts of castle walls and wooden gates. I almost felt like I had walked into a Shakespeare movie.

When I was a good distance into the room, the door shut behind me, and I was left in darkness. "Naomi? C'mon, please talk to me. What's going on?"

Something cranked from across the room, and then a spotlight blinded my vision as it pointed right at me. I raised my hand to shield myself from the light. "Naomi? This isn't funny anymore. Just turn on the lights so we can talk."

"So talk," Naomi's voice said behind me.

I turned to look at my friend. She was seated in a golden throne that had ornamental decorations all over the arms and back. Behind her stood several students and behind them was a brick wall with the sign that read "Brackenbury Lane" with an arrow pointing to the left.

I let out a short laugh when I realized it was the same brick wall where room 001 was supposed to be in the dungeon. The wall *was* fake. *That's* why Naomi didn't want me to knock on the bricks! Because I would've realized it wasn't real!

In Naomi's hand was the mask that was in her book bag, but she didn't put it on. Instead, she tossed it off to the side. And when I focused on the shadowed students behind her, I couldn't see their faces, but I knew the other kids weren't wearing their masks either.

I had never felt more betrayed in my life. "What is this? Please tell me this is a joke."

"You weren't supposed to find out yet," Naomi said.

"Don't say that," I said, feeling my heart break. "This whole thing is just a big dumb prank, isn't it? A big dumb prank that's lasted for over two weeks, right?"

Naomi didn't say anything.

"Come on!" I said. "This isn't real! You're not a Scavenger! You're my friend! You're one of my best ninjas! You're *afraid* of the Scavengers! You were so paranoid when I got their notes! You kept telling me to stay away from them! They even aired out *your* secrets!"

"All necessary for you to believe I was on your team," Naomi said. "Besides, those are secrets I don't care if anyone knows. So I had a crush on you – big whoop."

I shook my head at her, feeling a knot in my throat that wouldn't go down. "No, this isn't real. This isn't you!"

"Like I said," Naomi started, "you weren't supposed to find out… *yet.*"

"I don't believe you," I said, pointing at the kids behind Naomi. "None of you guys are wearing those vulture masks. If you were all Scavengers, then you'd all be working hard to hide your identity!"

Naomi LOL'd, as did the rest of the Scavengers behind her. "The masks were a joke," she explained. "It was all part of the act to scare you. Nobody here cares about hiding their identity. We're all pretty good at keeping secrets," she said with a wink. "We just found those masks in one of the drama club boxes and thought it'd be funny to wear them."

"No!" I shouted, refusing to believe her. "Stop this right now! This is a joke that's not funny! If you're working with the Scavengers, then that means you've been trashing my life this whole week! It means you've *helped* them do this to me! And that's not something I can believe!" I grew angrier. "Naomi, we're *friends!*"

"Chase," Naomi said. "I'm not *helping* them… I'm the *leader* of the Scavengers. *I'm* the one giving the orders!"

I felt the weight of everything press on my shoulders. It was too heavy for me to carry anymore, and I dropped me to my knees. "Since when?" I asked.

"Since the first day of school," Naomi answered honestly.

"No," I said. "You've been a member of my ninja clan the whole time."

"Doesn't it make sense then that the Scavengers would have a spy in your ninja clan?" Naomi said. "But remember at the time it was still Wyatt's clan. I wouldn't be the leader of the Scavengers if I *didn't* have my hand in everyone's cookie jar."

"Did Wyatt know?"

Naomi laughed. "That kid is the most clueless twerp in the school. Of course he didn't know!"

119

I felt like my brain was melting. I've known Naomi since the second week of school. How was it even possible that I didn't see this? How could I have missed something so huge? There's no way she was *that* good, was there?

"But I don't understand," I said. "You helped me bust Sebastian last week…"

Naomi shook her head. "No I didn't. You did that on your own. You figured out his entire plan by yourself. I did nothing to help you."

"But you didn't do anything to *stop* me," I said.

"I told you to stay out of it!" Naomi replied. "If I said anything more than that, I would've risked being discovered!"

I couldn't help myself, stepping forward and pointing an accusing finger at the girl I *used* to be friends with. "*Was this your plan the entire time?*"

The students around Naomi flinched, ready to stop me if I moved any closer.

Naomi held her hand up calmly, telling them to relax. "Don't worry, he's harmless. He wouldn't hurt a fly." She looked at me. "To be honest with you, the last two weeks have been quite a ride for me too. For the first time since the beginning of the year, I didn't know what to expect, but I knew things were changing and it was exciting. After you got Sebastian fired, we needed to replace him with another Scavenger."

"That's why you wanted to recruit me," I said. "And you were by my side the whole time *pretending* to be my friend."

"We seriously wanted you to join us, but when you rejected our offer to make you president," Naomi said, "we had to go with another student."

I thought for a moment. "Daisy…"

"There's no need to hide the truth from you anymore," Naomi said. "So yes, Daisy was your replacement. When we offered her a place with us, she jumped at the chance, which is what I was hoping *you* would've done. And now she's winning the election and another Scavenger will become the president of Buchanan School."

"I guess it's true what they say," I said.

The Scavengers glanced at each other, shrugging their shoulders.

120

Finally, Naomi spoke. "Are you going to finish that thought?"

"Oh right," I said. "Keep your friends close, but your enemies closer. You did a pretty good job of keeping me closer."

"Chase!" Naomi said, sitting forward with a smile on her face. "*I'm* not your enemy! I want you to join the Scavengers! It's not too late! You're an *amazing* ninja, but you'd make a better Scavenger!"

I stared at the girl in the throne. The girl who I thought I could trust. The girl who used to be one of my closest friends up until about ten minutes ago. "You've gone too far," I whispered. "You've killed my social life."

Naomi slammed her fist into the arm of her throne. "You left me no choice! I had to take everything from you!"

"*But why?*" I shouted.

"So you'd be left with no other option than to join us," Naomi said. She lifted her hand to the Scavengers around her again. "Step out of the shadows, guys."

Naomi's followers did as she ordered, shuffling forward at the same time.

I couldn't believe what I was seeing. The Scavengers that were behind her... were the members of my ninja clan.

"It's hard being a good leader," Naomi said. "Especially when you're never around."

I looked at one of the boys in front. He was the one I was speaking to back in the voting room. "But you just helped me get away from Jake and Wyatt."

The boy lowered his head and spoke with the same tone that he used before, not sad, but soft. "We're not against you, but we're not with you anymore. You've been absent from our training for far too long."

"Uh, duh!" I said, annoyed. "Because I've had loads of trouble I was trying to get rid of! It's like I'm juggling disasters every week!"

"We saved you from Jake and Wyatt," the boy said, "but that was the last time. We owed you at least that much."

I started to respond, but Naomi spoke louder to overpower my voice.

"You haven't been to training for over two weeks!" Naomi

121

said. "And before that, you'd show up maybe once a week! These kids – these *ninjas* wanted you to lead them! But you were never there."

I wanted to argue, but I couldn't. She was right. I'd been so busy trying to save the school that I hardly showed up to ninja training. And between the situation with Sebastian and the Scavengers, I knew I had completely dropped the ball.

All I could do was apologize. "I'm sorry."

"Nobody's mad at you," Naomi said softly. "But I could see your ninjas needed direction so I'm giving it to them."

The whole thing was still blowing my mind. Not only had Naomi served me a piping hot dish of *betrayal*, but it was also came with a cold glass of *take-all-my-ninja-clan-right-out-from-under-my-nose.* Yet she was speaking to me as if I was supposed to see this as a good thing!

It was like the way some people break up with their girlfriends by saying they're excited at how good of friends they'll be. Yeah right, those two never speak to each other ever again after that!

"Join us," Naomi said. "You can end this."

"You know I can't do that," I replied, staring at the floor.

"Then stay out of our way," Naomi said, and then she added, "Or we'll tell the school that you're a ninja. And don't even *think* about telling anyone about us or we'll put them through everything you've been through."

I sighed, realizing that was the exact moment that Naomi and I weren't going to be friends anymore. I said nothing else as I walked back to the exit.

"Once you walk out that door," Naomi said from behind me. "The invitation expires."

Without another thought, I stepped through the door and into the hallway. I heard it latch shut behind me, and I was alone again.

Friday. 7:30 AM. The cafeteria.

My dad had to drop me off early the next morning because the last part of my detention was to help clean the cafeteria after breakfast.

I dragged my feet across the floor, sliding a mop back and forth in front of me. I barely slept a wink overnight. I just couldn't get my mind off Naomi and the Scavengers plus all the other million things that had blown up in my face all week.

Since I'm such a pessimistic fool, I let my mind wander, thinking about what exactly happened this week.

First, the Scavengers offered me a place in their looney club. Rejecting them was the clap that started the avalanche.

They put my name into the pot for presidency, which is what angered Zoe at first, but claiming her pizza party for my own was what turned her anger into hatred. Since Gavin was her boyfriend, he obviously wasn't too happy with me either.

Brayden hated me too because of the video that the whole school saw. He was so embarrassed of it that he dropped out of the race. My face twitched at the thought of Brayden *quitting* something because of how ashamed he was. I felt so bad about it even though it wasn't my fault.

And then came the love notes that had been printed in that gossip newspaper. That was just the icing on the cake. That was how the Scavengers made it so that *everyone* hated me, and could you blame them?

But what hurt the most was that one of my best friends

turned out to be someone they weren't. Naomi was someone I could trust – someone I could tell my secrets to – someone I could count on to watch my back… and now that was gone.

The Naomi I knew was dead to me. No, that's not right – the Naomi I knew *never* existed. I thought about all those times she was by my side when Wyatt was being a butt, or when I needed to check out a hunch. All those times, she was simply following me, *spying* on me.

Betrayed by someone I trusted… bleh.

My thoughts went back to the ninja story I was daydreaming about earlier in the week – the one where I was on Scrag Seven rescuing Gwen from imprisonment.

I stopped mopping, remembering how my daydream turned out.

"Chase?" Zoe's voice said.

Glancing over my shoulder, I saw my cousin along with Gavin, Brayden, and Faith. "Hi," I said, plopping my mop back into its bucket.

Zoe paused, looking at everyone else. Finally, she spoke. "There's no way to do this without it being weird, but we all want to talk to you."

"Before you do," I said, "I just want to apologize. Guys, I'm *so so* sorry about this whole week."

"That's what we wanted to talk to you about," Zoe said, speaking for everyone. "It's obvious that there's something going on with you, and even though you've been a total dork all week, well… we want you to know that we're still going to be there for you."

"But why?" I asked, looking at the floor. "Why bother with me? I'm a lost cause. Everyone hates me."

Zoe leaned over so she could look me in the eye. "Because *that's* what friends do. Friends make mistakes, and friends forgive. I'm not going to go into an 'after-school-special' style speech for you to understand so don't make it weird. Just accept it and let's move forward."

I looked at Gavin, Brayden, and Faith. They nodded at me in return. Did I cry? No. Did I feel tears start to form in my eyes? …maybe.

"Friendship means understanding when mistakes are made,"

Zoe said. "You've made some monster mistakes this week, but we all feel the same way about it: the week wasn't the same without you around to joke with. So would you stop making those mistakes and be cool again?"

And like that, some of the weight lifted off my shoulders. I didn't feel as alone or helpless as I did earlier. My face practically split in half at how big my smile was.

I remembered Naomi's threat about ruining my friend's lives like she did with mine. And then, almost like she had planned it, I saw her peering through the tinted glass windows at the side of the cafeteria. She must've known what we were talking about because she put her finger to her lips and shook her head. Creepy much?

"All I can say is that everything that's happened this week," I said to my friends, "wasn't from me."

Brayden stepped forward. He had a smile on his face that I was glad to see. "I *knew* it! I *knew* you weren't evil enough to make a video like that!"

I burst out laughing, almost explosively. For the first time all week, I felt normal again. "That's all I can say though," I said. "At least for now."

Zoe folded her arms. "This is dumb. Just *tell* us what's going on already. You've really been a jerk this whole time, and I think you owe us an explanation!"

I nodded. "You're right, but I just... I can't. Please, believe me when I say I *want* to tell you."

My cousin shook her head, disappointed. "Fine. Be that way. Whatever it is can wait. Right now we have a cafeteria to clean."

Everyone grabbed some cleaning supplies and started wiping down tables and sweeping the floors.

When Faith and I were far from the group, she smiled at me. "Rough time this week, huh?"

I nodded. "You don't know the half of it."

"Maybe I know *something* about it," she said. "Secrets are hard to keep in this school."

"You're tellin' me," I said. "How much do you know?"

"Enough to know you're not the one pulling the strings on your campaign," Faith said. "It's like you're a marionette or something, getting pulled left and right without any power to stop it."

I glanced back at the tinted windows to make sure Naomi wasn't still watching. I couldn't see her anywhere. "But… how do you know?"

"It wasn't easy to figure out."

"Unless you were following me around the school, you couldn't possible know about all I've been through," I said.

Faith winked as she walked away. "Let's just say you're not the only one with a secret identity as a ninja."

"No, I'm sure I'm—" I stopped. "Wait, what?"

Faith didn't turn around.

Smirking, I watched until she was out of sight. Was I just talking to the white ninja? No way, right? There's *no way*, right?

I slapped the wet mop on the floor and dragged it back and forth. I guess only time will tell if she is or she isn't. Good thing I'm a patient dude.

Friday. 12:05 PM. The gymnasium.

The rest of the morning breezed by, mostly because I knew my closest friends were *still* my closest friends. Things might be awkward between Brayden and me, but hopefully that'll pass too.

I ate lunch by myself in the lobby by choice since I didn't feel like getting food thrown at my face again, especially since I was going to have to sit with the other candidates during the assembly.

As I stepped into the gymnasium, I realized that I hadn't seen Melvin, the reporter all day. I was so distracted by my friend's forgiveness that I totally forgot he had an article to publish with my ugly mug at the top of it. I had no doubt in my mind that he had pics of me getting unmasked by Jake.

It was the story he'd been hunting for all week. If I didn't at least try to explain myself to him, then I'd regret it. Hopefully he's a cool kid, and would decide against publishing the article. If my life was bad *before* my secret was revealed, just imagine what it was going to be like *afterward*.

Seriously, my parents would probably huddle together in the corner crying about where they went wrong. About where they could've tried harder. Or about whether it was too late to put me up for adoption.

Chairs were set up at the front of the gym like they had been on Monday during the assembly, except there was one extra chair on the end with my name taped to the seat. I think they forgot Brayden dropped from the race, which meant an empty seat

127

between Zoe and me.

In front of the chairs was the same podium that Principal Davis was setting up with the help of some kids from the tech club.

To the right side of the podium was a huge red machine that looked like something from a 70's science fiction movie. There was a slot in the top and one on the side. Under the side slot was a set of buttons that looked like they were taken from an old arcade game. I wasn't sure what the machine was for, but I was sure I'd find out during the assembly.

"Coopster for president!" shouted one of the students as he took a seat on the bleachers. The boys around him cheered my name too. Weird – I guess *not* everyone in the school hated me.

Some of the kids behind them were holding signs with my name painted on them.

"Aren't you guys mad that I gave away everyone's secrets?" I asked.

One of the blond haired boys stood and put his hand on my shoulder. "The school would be a better place if kids didn't keep secrets! Especially because I learned that the girl I had a crush on felt the same way!"

The girl next to him smiled at me.

"Oh, that's why you guys are cool with all that," I said. "You're all the kids who benefited from that gossip paper."

Everyone in the section cheered simultaneously, but I couldn't bring myself to be happy about them because it was still wrong. I waved my hand though. I mean, c'mon, when was the next time I was going to have any fans?

At the front of the gym, the other candidates were taking their seats on the metal chairs. As I sped my pace to join them, I spotted Naomi at the other end of the room, sitting in the first spot on the bleachers. She had been watching me the entire time, waiting for me to see her.

She raised her eyebrows at me. It was her way of giving me one final warning before the assembly started.

All I had to do was take my place up front and keep my

mouth shut. Daisy would win the election, the Scavengers would have their president, and I could just disappear in the school until I graduate.

If you would've asked me at the beginning of the year if that sounded nice, I would've said yes. But things have been different for me in the past few months. Things have gotten better, and I've changed. I didn't *want* to get lost in the crowd anymore.

I sat on my seat up front, watching all the kids in the gym. I don't know the official count of how many sixth graders there were at Buchanan School, but there must have been hundreds. Nearly every spot on the bleachers were taken.

Zoe leaned over the empty spot between us. "This is exciting, isn't it? In a short time, we'll find out who the new president of Buchanan is!" She crossed her fingers, giggling. "Listen, if *you* win, we're still cool, okay? I'd rather you win than Wyatt."

Wyatt slouched forward to see past Daisy. "Don't count on it, losers. Get used to hearing 'President Wyatt' because that's all you're going to hear after today."

"That doesn't make sense," Zoe said, rolling her eyes.

"Yes it does!" Wyatt said.

Daisy said nothing, sitting perfectly still with her hands folded on her lap. She was staring into space. If it wasn't for her shoulders rising with each breath, I could've mistaken her for a porcelain doll.

I studied her, feeling anxious for the assembly to start. She knew she was going to win this thing. It was promised to her by the Scavengers. It probably felt pretty good to be a hundred percent certain of victory.

"But if *I* win," Zoe said, snapping me out of my gaze. "Then I'd love it if you helped me with my role. You fumbled this week when you couldn't be my campaign manager, but that's behind us."

My cousin was so good at making me feel terrible without knowing it. She was being so cool by forgiving me and asking me to help after she won.

Too bad she wasn't going to win. Maybe that's why I felt terrible.

Oh well. For the sake of my ninja secret, it was time to push

130

those emotions down to the deepest part of my stomach.

I looked once more for Melvin. There were a lot of kids in the gym so I wasn't sure I'd even see him at all. It was like trying to find that guy in the red and white striped sweatshirt and hat – *frustrating and impossible!* What's he doing in overcrowded places to begin with?

Principal Davis strolled to the podium. He tapped it twice and said, *"What's up, Buchanan Meese?"*

Everyone cheered because he was making fun of the fact that "moose" is plural for "moose," so even when we're referring a bunch of those animals, it still sounded like we were just talking about one. Calling us the "Buchanan *Meese*" was becoming a popular joke.

Tapping on the red machine next to the podium, the principal continued. "In just a few moments we're going to use this vote counter to print out the results of the election! It's a state of the art machine called the 'BOJO 2015!' Don't ask me what it means 'cause I don't know."

I leaned toward my cousin. "Don't we need to vote first?"

Zoe looked at me like I was an idiot. "Everyone voted during lunch. Didn't you?"

"Uhhhh," I groaned, sinking down like my body was turning to mush.

"*You didn't vote?*" Zoe whispered harshly.

I smiled, but it was forced. "Whoopsies."

"Man, if I lose by *one* vote, I'm going to be so upset with you!"

Leaning back in my chair, I stared at the red machine that Principal Davis was resting his arm on. How was Naomi going to rig the election? They were using a machine to count the votes, but was it possible that she found a way to hack into it?

Daisy sat in the empty seat next to mine. "Hello, Chase."

I glanced at Zoe, who was distracted with watching the crowd.

"Daisy," I said, looking away.

"This will all be over shortly," she said, bravely speaking aloud while sitting between my cousin and me. "All you have to do is absolutely nothing. That's easy enough for you, right?"

Her words cut into my heart.

"How's it feel to finally fail?" Daisy asked.

Now she was just twisting the knife. "Leave me alone," I said.

"Maybe after this I will. Or maybe I won't. Maybe this has been the most excitement I've had my entire life, and maybe I won't let up on you," Daisy sneered. "Maybe I've enjoyed watching you squirm as Naomi held you over the fire. And maybe this is just the beginning of a beautiful war between the Scavengers and you."

"Maybe you say 'maybe' too much," I said.

"Maybe," Daisy said one last time.

Principal Davis slapped the top of the vote counting machine. For some reason it wasn't working properly, probably from being such an ancient gadget.

I wanted to tell Daisy that she wasn't going to get away with this – that *none* of the Scavengers would, but what good was it? They *were* going to pull it off without anyone knowing any better. Anyone except me.

Even if I *did* say something, it's not like I had any kind of proof. It's not like I could stand up in front of everyone and start telling them about the Scavengers and their plan to rig the election. The principal would look at me and be like, "How do you know?"

What would my answer be? "Because I just know!" isn't good enough! I would look like a crazy person. Not only that but it would look like I was being a sore loser since I'm *in* the election!

The Scavengers seemed to have every corner covered, and it was sickening to me. No wonder why Naomi was such a good ninja – because she was an even better Scavenger.

Finally, the red machine spit out a long sheet of paper. Principal Davis caught it in the air before it landed on the ground. Holding the results in front of his face, he squinted so he could read the fine print.

A smile appeared on the principal's face as he tapped the microphone again.

Daisy had returned to her seat next to Wyatt. She was sitting straight up with her eyes half closed.

Wyatt was scanning his victory speech, moving his lips as he recited it to himself.

Zoe had her eyes squeezed shut. Her fingers were crossed as she held them next to her face, and her legs were bouncing up and down.

My cousin wanted to win so badly. I had to look away from her because I knew what was about to happen. I didn't want to see the moment her heart broke.

Principal Davis let out of puff of air through his nose. "Buchanan Meese, I'm pleased to present to you the winner of the election by a *landslide…*"

The crowd fell silent, eagerly awaiting the results.

Something had to happen right? The bad guys don't win in situations like this, do they? My heart was pounding in my chest as I stared at the principal. Come on! Please say that someone else had won! I'd even accept *Wyatt* as president if it meant the Scavengers didn't win!

The principal paused. And then he shouted loudly into the mic. "Give a big round of applause for *President Daaaaaisy!*"

Zoe tried keeping her composure, but I saw her body sink ever so slightly. A smile appeared on her face, but I knew there was a world of sadness behind it.

I bit my lip as Daisy stood from her chair. She clapped both hands in front of her chest like a cheerleader. Then she mouthed the words "Thank you," as she started waving to the cheering crowd of sixth graders.

Balloons and confetti drifted down from the ceiling of the gymnasium at the same time that music started playing over the sound system. The Scavengers had won and the presidency would continue to remain in their clutches.

How? How could this have happened?

From the bleachers, I saw Naomi staring at me. Not angry – just staring. I'm not sure why, but the story of Gwen, the queen of Scrag Seven, started replaying in my mind.

The prisoner I had rescued on Scrag turned out to be not just the villain, but the ultimate villain – the *queen*. Someone I had trusted, someone who was helping me, someone who was fighting by my side and then *betrayed* me.

All of humanity was going to be enslaved if the queen wasn't stopped. And now all of Buchanan School was going to continue being led by a Scavenger.

I saved the Earth in the story by sacrificing myself, tackling the queen. Obviously tackling Naomi wasn't going to save the day, but...

My brain lit up as my blood surged through my veins.

I could fix this.

I could change the election. I didn't have solid evidence, but if I told the school a secret so huge that their minds would explode, then maybe, just *maybe* I could bring enough attention to the Scavengers that Principal Davis would *have* to investigate!

But it meant that I had to sacrifice myself.

The only power the Scavengers had over me was the fact that Buchanan School didn't know I was a ninja.

Well that was about to change.

Daisy was at the center of the gym, shaking hands and getting her picture taken when I walked up to the podium.

"Hello?" I said into the mic, checking to see if it was still on. My voice came through loud and clear over the speakers.

Principal Davis stood behind me. "Chase, what're you doing?"

"I'd like to address the students," I said. "I'd like to apologize for all the junk that's happened this week."

The principal thought for a moment. "I think that's appropriate, but keep it short."

"Roger roger," I said, tapping the microphone with my finger. "Um, hello?"

Everyone in the gym slowly fell silent. All eyes were on me. Even Naomi's. It was right at that moment when I saw Melvin step through the doors.

Good, I thought. At least when he prints his story, everyone will be ready to believe it.

I cleared my throat, aware of the several hundred students staring at me. Most of those kids hated me, but in just a few seconds they were going to hate me even more.

Was I about to do the dumbest thing I've ever done? This

was a life changing decision that would follow me through to graduation. I'll be forever remembered as "that-weirdo-ninja-kid."

Glancing over my shoulder, I saw Zoe. And in that instant, I knew I was about to do the right thing.

Admitting to the school that I was a ninja was only going to be the beginning. The domino effect would continue until the Scavengers were revealed, and then continue further until Daisy's victory was exposed to be a lie. It was the right thing to do. There wasn't even an inch of me that thought otherwise.

"First of all," I said, "I'd like to apologize to everyone for any kind of stress or heartache that the Chase Cooper Newsletter might've put you through. If I could go back in time and burn all those gossip papers, I totally would."

Naomi slowly lifted her head, listening carefully. She was still in the same spot at the side of the gym.

"I know I'm normally the shy quiet guy who sits in the back of class. A few of you might recognize me from some bizarre antics I've been apart of since I started school here," I said. "I'll tell you exactly why I was involved in those antics. It's because

I've been living two lives…"

I heard Wyatt squirm in his seat behind me.

Zoe gasped, and whispered, "*What are you doing?*"

But I ignored her and continued speaking. "One life that everyone knows about as a sixth grader at Buchanan, but the other life is a secret, filled with darkness and shadows…"

The gym was so silent that if I shut my eyes, I would swear it was empty. To make it easier, I actually *did* shut my eyes.

"You see," I said, before pausing. My hands were trembling like leaves, and my knees felt like they had teleported away from my body.

I was about to do it. About to let the school know I was a ninja that had a secret ninja clan. About to take away all the power the Scavengers had over me. About to ruin my own life.

"You see," I repeated, my voice shaking. I took a deep breath. "I'm a nin—"

"*Waaaait!*" screeched a voice in the gymnasium.

My heart was still in my belly when I squinted to see who was running toward the podium.

It was Melvin. His brown loafers squeaked on the floor as he stomped toward the front of the gym, waving around sheets of paper over his head. "Stop! I have something to say!"

"I'm kind of in the middle of something," I said into the mic.

Melvin ignored me, pushing me away from the podium. Holding the papers over his head, he said, "I have *proof* that Daisy rigged the election! She should *not* be the president!"

"Those are pretty strong words," Principal Davis said angrily as he covered the mic with his hand.

Melvin held out the sheets of paper. They were photographs that he had taken when we were in the voting room. Daisy was in the background of the first picture, but the rest of the pictures were zoomed closer to see what she was actually doing.

Under his stack of photos were the pink slips that Melvin had taken from the voting room. They were the slips of paper that fell out of the box Daisy was holding over the red machine. The same red machine that was sitting next to the podium. The vote counting machine.

"Tell me," Melvin said, pointing to the results sheet that the red machine had printed. "Does it say Daisy won because she got the vote of *every* homeschooled kid in the district?"

Principal Davis furrowed his brow, but checked the results like Melvin had asked. Then his expression softened. "Actually yes, you're right. It does."

"Those homeschooled kids *don't* exist!" Melvin said loud enough that his voice was carried through the speakers. "Daisy rigged the election by winning a ton of votes from fake people! These pink slips are votes from homeschoolers, but when I looked up their names, I found out they weren't even real! The machine makes sure that there aren't any duplicate names from any of the voters, but it doesn't count *similar* names as the same! Look!" Melvin pointed at the names on a couple of the pink slips. "*John* Doe. *Jon* Doe! I mean, come on, really? Daisy was dumping these votes into the voting machine *before* anyone even voted!"

Principal Davis's voice remained unchanged as he studied the pink slips in Melvin's hand. Then he stepped up to the mic. With a calm voice, he said, "Daisy, please go to the front office. I'll be there in a few minutes to have some words with you."

I could hear gasps in the crowd. Whispers of how dead meat she was drifted through too.

Principal Davis stood in a huddle with several other teachers. They were whispering to each other and pointing at the photos and pink slips that Melvin had brought in.

I looked at the reporter who was leaning against the podium.

"Don't worry about it," Melvin said, answering my "thank you" before I even said it. He leaned away from the mic. "You saved me yesterday. This was the least I could do for you."

I nodded.

"Besides," Melvin added. "A rigged election is way more exciting than ninjas."

Finally, Principal Davis took the podium again. "I'm sorry to say that the results for the presidency were skewed, but after much discussion with the rest of the staff, we believe that the student who came in *second* place should be the winner. That and I think we're all so exhausted from how crazy the week has been that we just want to get a new president and move on."

I stepped back and glanced at Zoe. In a fair election, she

was definitely going to be the winner.

"Chase Cooper," Principal Davis said, "You received the second most votes, which makes you the *next* president of Buchanan School!"

My jaw dropped, and I think most of the sixth graders felt the same. There were mixed reactions mumbling back and forth. The section of students that were happy about the Chase Cooper Newsletter jumped to their feet, roaring with applause.

Principal Davis torqued his head. "But wait, what were you saying earlier? You're a nin-what?"

I paused, my jaw still hanging on its hinges. "Nincompoop," I said. "I was *going* to say that I'm a nincompoop, and that I was going to respectfully bow out of the race."

"I see," the principal said. "Well, since you're the winner, I'm sure you've changed your mind."

I looked at Zoe. Now that Daisy was out of the way, I was going to be the president, but if *I* were out of the way, I know the position would've landed on Zoe because I'm sure Wyatt probably only got one vote, and that would've been from Olive.

I'm sure you'd love to hear me say I made the "right" choice, but to me, it was *never* a choice. Zoe *deserved* the presidency more than anyone in the entire school.

It doesn't matter though because she was the student who genuinely won. Daisy cheated. I was only elected because the Scavengers tossed my name into the hat. I shouldn't even have been in the race to begin with.

"No sir," I said to the principal, without taking my eyes off my cousin. "I haven't changed my mind at all. I respectfully withdraw my name from the ballot."

The principal rubbed the bridge of his nose, annoyed. "Seriously, what's wrong with the kids at this school?" he mumbled. Then he scanned the voting results. He was too wiped to sound excited anymore. Leaning into the mic for a final time, he quickly said, "Zoe is the new president of the school, and *that's* that."

"I demand a recount!" Wyatt shouted as he stood.

The principal tossed the results to Wyatt. "Count 'em yourself. You got *zero* votes."

Wyatt studied the sheet of paper. "*Olive* didn't even vote for me?"

My cousin threw her arms around my body, almost knocking me to the floor. She was so happy that she couldn't say a word, but I knew what she wanted to say.

"You're welcome," I said. "I couldn't be there for you as a campaign manager, but I hope this makes up for that."

She nodded. "It does, but don't forget that I'm still going to need your help while I'm president so don't think you dodged a bullet with this."

"I don't expect anything less from you," I smirked.

Zoe took the podium and waved to the sixth graders. They cheered loudly for her as she started giving her acceptance speech.

I looked over at Naomi, but she wasn't on the bench anymore.

Deep down, I knew that I had just declared war with the Scavengers, but I couldn't let myself think about it. There was too much to celebrate.

Melvin had a better story to print, and he wasn't going to reveal my secret. My friends were still my friends even after I was a butthead to them. And my cousin was the new president of Buchanan. For such a disastrous week, it turned out better than I expected.

The Scavengers said that every president had been a Scavenger since Buchanan first opened its door. Without the presidency, they were beginning to lose their grip of control, and that felt awesome to me. Even though my week was a double decker bus of catastrophe, taking the Scavengers down a notch was worth it.

But I also knew that it wasn't the last time I'd run into them. They were able to wreck my life in less than a week! I wasn't looking forward to seeing what they were capable of with more time.

As Zoe spoke about the future of Buchanan, I took my seat behind her, listening as she transformed into the leader she was born to be.

Daisy was somewhere in the principal's office by now.

Wyatt was off to the side of the gym, sitting next to Olive, but they were facing away from each other. Wyatt was pouting with his arms folded as Olive rolled her eyes repeatedly.

Brayden was sitting with Gavin and Faith, clapping at Zoe's every other sentence.

Melvin was about five feet in front of the podium, taking photos of Zoe for the school paper.

The school only knows where Naomi ran off to.

And me? I was perfectly happy being in the background as my cousin took the spotlight. Ninjas are at their best when they're neither seen nor heard. And at least for a little longer, my secret was safe from the school.

My eyes caught Melvin's one last time. He simply nodded, at which I returned the gesture. Without a ninja clan, I'd have to begin recruiting soon, but this time I'd be more careful about who I picked. Because Melvin's a reporter, he'd be a good addition – reporters have the best connections.

The Scavengers *would* be back, but I just didn't know when. It could be Monday, a week from now, a month from now. I just didn't know. So there was no sense in wasting time. If I wanted to be ready for them, I'd have to start building a ninja clan, and soon.

I took a deep breath – deeper than normal. Then I held it for a second. Zoe had just said something that excited the school, and the gymnasium erupted with applause. The sound of cheering students flooded my ears, making it easier to clear my head. At last, I exhaled slowly, feeling all the weight from the week leave me.

Good thing it was Friday because my brain had just checked out for the weekend. All I wanted was to plop down in front of my video games with a stack of comic books by my side, drinking a frosty mug of orange soda with two scoops of vanilla ice cream in it. It might sound lame-o to you, but it sounded like the perfect weekend for me.

Zoe's speech was coming to an end as she said, "I'm going to put in the hours and work weekends to be the best president I

144

can be. I'm not even going to waste time telling all of you how I'll be different from Sebastian because I believe true leadership *isn't* about being better than the other guy…"

Um… was my own cousin about to gank my line?

Zoe winked at me, and finished her speech. "It's about always trying to be better than *yourself*."

I laughed. Yup. She totally took that from me.

Stories — what an incredible way to open one's mind to a fantastic world of adventure. It's my hope that this story has inspired you in some way, lighting a fire that maybe you didn't know you had. Keep that flame burning no matter what. It represents your sense of adventure and creativity, and that's something nobody can take from you. Thanks for reading! If you enjoyed this book, I ask that you help spread the word by sharing it or leaving an honest review!

- Marcus
m@MarcusEmerson.com

THESE BOOKS ARE MORE AWESOME THAN TWO SCOOPS OF VANILLA ICE CREAM IN A FROSTY MUG OF ORANGE SODA! HAVE YOU EVER HAD THAT? IF NOT, THEN YOU SHOULD TRY IT BECAUSE IT TASTES **SUPER AWESOME!**